Marrying Miss Milton

Brides of Brighton Book 2

ASHTYN NEWBOLD

Copyright © 2018 by Ashtyn Newbold
All rights reserved.

No part of this book may be reproduced in any form whatsoever, whether by graphic, visual, electronic, film, microfilm, tape recording, or any other means, without prior written permission of the publisher, except in the case of brief passages embodied in critical reviews and articles.

This is a work of fiction. The characters, names, incidents, places and dialogue are products of the author's imaginations and are not to be construed as real. Any resemblance of characters to any person, living or dead, is purely coincidental.

ISBN 13: 9781075320460

Editing by Tori MacArthur

Front cover design by Blue Water Books

*For the kindhearted and brave.
You inspire me.*

Chapter 1

ENGLAND, AUTUMN, 1813

The eyes of Jane Milton's father held every sign of a well-kept secret. She observed him carefully from across the dining table, the bright morning sun casting his face in shadow. His lips pressed together to contain any words that might escape his mouth without permission, avoiding the risk of spilling the secret that lurked in his eyes. Jane knew the secret to be a positive thing, for despite his effort to hold his expression, she glimpsed a smile pulling at his cheeks.

"Please, Papa! Tell me!" She cast her fork back onto her plate, letting the scrambled eggs cushion its fall. As she surveyed the rest of the table, she found that her mother and young brother carried the same looks of suspicion.

"There is nothing to tell, my dear," Jane's father said, breaking the seemingly permanent seal of his lips to take a bite of bread. "Please do sit in your chair."

Jane released a huffed breath. She had not realized she had stood.

Reclaiming her seat at the table, she glanced down at her plate, the food there not nearly as appetizing as the hidden knowledge her family kept from her. She had always despised being left out. But it was not a rare thing for her, unfortunately, so she knew how to endure it well.

Of the four Milton daughters, Jane was the oldest, and the only one yet to be married. Just the day before they had bid farewell to Abigail as she had ridden away with her new husband, an earl, no less. Jane's mother attributed her single state to her fearsome carrot-hued locks, and her father attributed it to her freckles. Her sisters willingly submitted that they thought her lack of a husband was in direct correlation with her inability to behave properly in social situations, and her brother, not twelve years of age, told her she ought to wear less rouge, for her complexion already burned a rosy color almost constantly.

But Jane knew her lack of attachment had less to do with all of these things, and more to do with the fact that she was helplessly in love with a man that had yet to notice her. For seven years she had been unable to imagine her future with any other but Henry Stone, Viscount of Barnet. Tall, dashing, brooding, and with the muscle of a greek god, Lord Barnet had stolen her heart the day he rode past her on his black horse when she had been fifteen years old, collecting flowers in the woods between their neighborhoods. She had never spoken to him, but the impression he had left on her young heart was irreplaceable.

Of course, her intense red hair and freckles did not aid her chance at marriage, but without Lord Barnet, Jane might have made an effort to be friendly and alert in social gatherings. She might have been aware of the men that surrounded her. But all of her attention would forever be captured by the mysterious viscount.

Jane's brother Harry gave a mischievous smile. "I know Papa's secret," he said around a mouthful of ham.

"What is it?" she asked in a whisper, leaning toward him. Her curiosity could not be contained.

"Harry, do not dare tell her!" Jane's mother held a finger to her lips, her eyes narrowing.

Jane's heart raced in anticipation. What could they be hiding from her?

Her father dabbed at his mouth with a napkin. "With Abigail's marriage complete, we are now completely devoted to finding a match for you, Jane," her father began. She stared into his eyes, the only feature she shared with her family. Every child had been born with the same blonde hair, crisp blue eyes, and fair, unblemished skin. Except Jane. She had inherited the eyes but had received wild ginger curls and freckled cheeks. Of course, she had been the last daughter her parents would seek a husband for, though she had been their firstborn.

"I am capable of finding my own match, thank you," Jane said.

She looked down at her plate in disappointment. Had that been the secret? Lord Barnet had already refused all of Jane's sisters, beginning with Emma, then Cecily, and finally Abigail. Jane had feigned illness each time he had come to call, avoiding the possibility that he would refuse her as well. She preferred clinging to the dream of him rather than facing the reality of his pending indifference to her. Yet she still hoped that when he did see her, he would return her affection. Until then, she didn't need her parents throwing men in her path that she didn't want.

"If you were capable of that, you would have found your own match already," her mother said.

Jane's jaw dropped with indignation. She started to protest but was stopped by a large piece of scone as it struck the side of her face.

"Harry!" she glared at her brother as he fell into a bout of laughter.

"I tried to throw it into your mouth."

"It is most impolite to hang your mouth agape in such a way, Jane," her mother scolded.

She gasped. "Is it not impolite to throw food at one's sister?"

"He is only a boy."

Jane glanced at her brother as he cast her a winning smile. But only she could see the mischief in it. The little scoundrel had managed to convince their parents that he was an angel.

"As you know, your sisters have all secured marriages with peers, a feat which Mr. Milton and I are most proud of." Jane's mother exchanged a broad smile with her husband, gratification glowing in her eyes. "Emma to an earl, Cecily to a baron, and Abigail to an earl as well. To have so many advantageous matches within one family is unheard of in all of Surrey. We hope to continue our legacy with you."

Yes, but Jane's sisters also possessed a *beauty* that was unheard of in all of Surrey. Jane simply could not compare. In recent years her maid had learned to tame her wild hair into something presentable, and Jane had learned to always use a bonnet out of doors to minimize her freckles. But that did not change the pestering fact that she was still the plainest and most undesirable Milton daughter.

"How do you intend to do that?" she asked in a bored voice.

Her parents shared a glance, that secret jumping to the surface of her father's eyes once again. Jane sat forward. Waiting. Hoping.

"As we discussed the matter after Abigail's wedding yesterday, we realized that the Viscount of Barnet has yet to meet you. We have invited him to dine with us this evening."

"Did you?" Jane put on a show of indifference while she choked on a breath. She had been waiting for this day with a mixture of dread and excitement. With her sisters now unavailable, there was a chance Lord Barnet might find it within his heart to notice her. She now had claim on the entire stage, without her talented and beautiful sisters to steal every spectating eye.

"Indeed," her father said, "and he has agreed to it. We shall receive him at six o'clock."

The room had blurred together as Jane's heart raced, the three faces across the table blending into one—the beard of her father, the jewelry of her mother, and the smirk of Harry.

"Are you well? You look quite pale." Jane's mother emerged in her vision, a scowl marking her brow.

"I am perfectly well, Mama. I—I was simply considering what I should wear this evening."

"You must wear your green taffeta with the white trim. It is the only gown you have hope of looking pretty enough in to catch his attention."

Jane nodded, her mother's words scratching through her like broken glass.

"And my hair?"

"I will leave that to Suzanne."

Jane swallowed her fear. Her maid always knew how to help her look presentable. But she would need to look more than presentable if she hoped to impress Lord Barnet. Her heart skittered in her chest. Could this really be happening? Jane could not believe it.

"I don't like Lord Barnet," Harry said. "He looks like this." Drawing his pale eyebrows together, Harry narrowed his eyes and tightened his jaw, glaring across the table.

It was true, Lord Barnet was quite serious in appearance, but that did not mean he couldn't *learn* to smile. His brooding, mysterious countenance captivated Jane, making her wonder what he could be like upon closer inspection. How boring he would be if he had nothing to hide.

She realized she had been gazing out the window, a silly smile plastered to her lips. Harry threw a slice of ham at her face, where it made a direct and wet impact with her chin.

"Harry!" She wiped ham juice from her chin and leapt to her feet, running around the table toward him.

"Jane!" Her mother scolded, slamming down her glass.

Harry scrambled out of his chair, racing out the dining room door, his giggles echoing against the walls. Jane chased him to the back door of the house and onto the grass, eventually finding herself joining in his laughter. She stopped to catch her breath, squinting against the sun as he continued running toward the woods.

Away from her family, she could finally comprehend what she had just discovered. Lord Barnet would really be joining them for dinner. Jane wanted to be excited, but a greater part of her was afraid.

Finding her way to her favorite tree on their property, tucked within the gardens, she lay down on the grass, propping her hand behind her head.

Her stomach twisted. She could not be a coward now. She had avoided Lord Barnet these years for fear of rejection. But how would she ever know if she had a chance if she did not act? Why should a man like Lord Barnet be opposed to her? She chewed her lip.

She could think of many reasons.

Shunning all negative thought, she stretched her back, yawning. She had hardly slept the night before, and the warm and comfortable grass was a stark reminder. Filling her lungs, she closed her eyes in deep meditation. Nothing could stop her from marrying Lord Barnet. She had dreamt of it for years. It was all she wanted. At the age of twenty-two with three perfect younger sisters, Jane had never had anything she wanted. A breeze ruffled the grass around her head, and she let out a sigh of contentment.

Perhaps her luck would finally turn.

Chapter 2

Jane awoke to the sound of thunder, cracking in the air, vibrating the ground she had been peacefully sleeping on. The moment she opened her eyes, a downpouring of rain came crashing through the tree above her, not even its dense leaves capable of containing it.

Scrambling to her feet, she covered her head with her hands. Water soaked through her morning dress and poured through her fingers and onto her hair and face. She shrieked, stumbling blindly out of the gardens and through the back door of the house. She caught her breath, staring out the window in fascination at the torrent that had stolen her nap from her. The sky churned in various shades of darkness, the clouds reminding Jane of a large gray towel being wrung dry of every drop it contained.

"Jane! I have been searching for you!" The sound of her mother's voice tore her gaze from the storm.

She turned around, shocked at her mother's fierce disposition.

"We were just informed that Lord Barnet has another commitment this evening. He means to come early!" Her mother's eyes widened in dismay at Jane's soaked appearance, grumbling something under her breath.

Jane's heart sank. "What is the time?"

"It is past four o'clock! He will be arriving in less than one hour."

Jane touched her hair, dread pouring through her. No. No. No. If her hair managed to dry in time for Lord Barnet's arrival it would be covered in frizz and untamable curl. If it remained wet she would look just as unattractive.

"Suzanne!" her mother called as she stomped up the staircase. Jane followed behind her. How had she slept for so long? The grass had been so warm and comfortable, and coupled with her trouble sleeping the night before, the combination had caused her to sleep almost the entire day.

When they reached Jane's bedchamber, Suzanne awaited her. Young and lively, Suzanne had a way of turning Jane's mood to one of hope. With a quick glance, the maid assessed the situation, starting with Jane's hair. Sitting Jane down in front of the looking glass, she removed every pin, leaving the wet tendrils to hang about Jane's face and shoulders. When her hair was wet, Jane liked the color much more. It transformed to a deep auburn rather than a fierce orange.

After giving instruction to Suzanne, Jane's mother left the room, muttering unholy words under her breath. Jane swallowed, watching her chest rise and fall in the mirror.

"Not to worry, miss. We will fix your hair in time for Lord Barnet. You will look ravishing, I am certain." Suzanne tugged on a strand, making Jane cringe.

Thirty minutes later, Jane's hair appeared just as it had before the storm, aside from a slight dampness. Suzanne had adorned the style with small pearls. She moved to pinch Jane's cheeks, but Jane stopped her. She would not need any assistance in adding color to her complexion tonight. The mere sight of Lord Barnet would likely set her face blazing.

Descending the staircase proved to be a difficult thing when walking upon shaking legs. Jane took a steadying breath. Lord Barnet would be arriving at any moment. She wore her green dress per her mother's instruction. When her parents met her at the base of the stairs, they greeted her with looks of appraisal.

"I suppose this will have to suffice." Jane's mother raised an eyebrow, straightening the ribbon at Jane's waist.

Jane tried to smile, but her lips were dry. How could she speak to Lord Barnet? She had only seen him from afar, taking his morning rides, perusing the shops in town, or through the window of her bedchamber on the days he had descended from his carriage to meet her sisters.

"Remember, you must maintain a smile at every moment, Jane. Your smile is your sharpest weapon."

Oh, yes. Her mother referred to features of beauty as 'weapons,' as if she were trying to instruct her daughters in how to injure a man rather than entice him.

Jane nodded, licking her lips before offering her best grin.

"Smaller," her father said, tilting his head.

Jane constricted her smile, closing her lips over her teeth. "Much better."

In the drawing room, Jane sat down between her mother and Harry, who still avoided Jane's gaze after his ham-throwing this morning. Her hands grew slick with perspiration. Would Lord Barnet clearly see her parents' motive for inviting him here? How embarrassing it would be if he did not pay any attention to her. She almost hoped he wouldn't. It would be much easier.

"He has arrived," her father said, moving from the window and taking a place on the settee.

Jane's heart gave a distinct leap.

An excruciating minute later, the front door clicked open at the hands of their butler, the hinges creaking with foreboding. Jane thought she might faint as the footman announced the name *Lord Barnet* at the entry of the drawing room. She stared at her hands, counting to three in her mind before daring to look up.

There he stood, in all his masculine glory, stealing every bit of light from the room with his presence, outshining every crystal of the chandelier above them. He wore green, unwittingly matching Jane's dress, and without a doubt intentionally matching his eyes. Jane caught his gaze—his beautiful gaze—and her heart all but stopped. The room spun, and she blinked twice.

Jane didn't notice her father stand to greet him until he crossed her line of sight. "Lord Barnet, we offer our sincere welcome to our home once again. We so enjoy your company."

Jane's mother joined them, throwing Jane a look of dismay when she remained on the sofa. Her mother cleared her throat, gesturing with her eyes for Jane to stand.

"Am I to be the only guest in attendance?" Lord Barnet asked, his brow creasing in a likeness to Harry's imitation that morning.

Her parents shared a look. "Oh ... our other guests were detained by family matters, unfortunately. You will be our only guest this evening."

Jane moved to her feet, still in a daze. Shaking herself back to consciousness, she walked across the room.

"Please meet my eldest daughter, Miss Jane Milton," her father said as she reached them. Jane found the eyes of Lord Barnet once again, the green of them shocking. He offered a slow nod that she returned.

"It is a pleasure to finally meet you," he said, echoing the thoughts that crossed through her mind. To Jane it was *more* than a pleasure to meet him. It was the product of her fondest dreams. She bit her tongue to keep from saying something similar to his face.

"You as well," she squeaked.

After a moment of brief conversation between Lord Barnet and her parents, he offered his arm to her as the small group moved to the dining room. Jane had nearly lost her mind at the prospect of speaking to him. To touch his arm? To risk creasing his perfectly smooth jacket? Without looking at his face, she laid her hand on his arm as if it were a fragile thing, not the sturdy, muscled thing that it was.

In the dining room, her father placed Lord Barnet strategically beside Jane at the corner of the table, and far from Harry. She praised the heavens in gratitude.

Jane's parents started the conversation, bringing Jane into the topic with ease. When the first course was served, she didn't dare eat her turnip soup and risk spilling it all over herself. Her hand shook as she lifted her spoon.

"Miss Milton, I wondered why I had not met you before this evening."

It took her a moment to realize Lord Barnet was speaking to her. She swallowed her soup, cringing as the hot liquid tore down her throat.

Her eyes watered as she took a sip from her goblet.

The water found its way to her airway instead, causing her lungs to protest in a fit of coughing. She set the goblet down on the table, bent over her napkin as her body heaved, dispelling the water from her lungs. Her face burned hotter than her turnip soup as Lord Barnet placed his hand on her back, patting between her shoulders as if to aid her cough, a pained look on his face.

Embarrassing as it was, the coughing added credibility to her next statement. She sat up, stammering an apology before rasping, "I found myself ill every time you came to our home. It was purely coincidental, of course."

"So I assumed."

Jane scolded herself for her pathetic excuse. To clarify that it had been coincidental only made her appear guiltier. She looked up from her soup, sensing his gaze on the side of her face.

Lord Barnet smiled. "It is a shame I did not have the privilege of meeting you sooner." His voice, low and gruff, sent shivers down her arms and his words set her pulse racing.

"But it's quite fortuitous that you have met her now, is it not?" Jane's mother said, her lips twisting in a coy smile.

"Indeed, it is," he said.

Jane watched him, hope rising in her heart. He did not seem at all opposed to spending more time with her. Her cheeks flushed, growing hot at the centers as she awaited his reply.

Lord Barnet wiped his mouth with his napkin. "But I'm afraid I will be unable to further my acquaintance with Miss Milton at the moment. I am leaving to Brighton on the morrow and will remain there through the autumn and winter months for the course of the social season."

"I see," Jane's father said, all rapture fading from his voice.

Jane's heart fell, disappointment sinking through her. Lord Barnet was leaving? How could he leave the very day after she was finally able to meet him? Eligible as he was, he could not spend a social season in Brighton and return unattached. So near the romantic beauty of the ocean, with social activities every evening, he was sure to find a woman in Brighton that he would like much better than Jane.

"I tire of spending the season in London each year," Lord Barnet said. "I thought my time might be better spent testing the social society of a new town. Brighton attracts a multitude of new visitors each year."

Her father nodded, his smile strained. "As I have heard."

Jane didn't want to sit at the table any longer. She had spent years dreaming of this day, only to have her dream shattered. She knew Brighton to be the seaside town the Prince Regent frequented, and the home of his royal pavilion. Why would Lord Barnet choose Brighton? The bulk of society still gathered in London each year. She did not want him to go to London either, for that could still bring about the same result: Jane would lose her chance with him forever.

The conversation turned to various topics that Jane did not care about. She sat in silence, chewing her bread angrily. Harry threw her a mocking smile from across the table, and she had to stop herself from throwing a grape at him.

When Lord Barnet took his leave, Jane hurried to the front window to watch his carriage drive away. She pressed her palm to the window, the cold glass reflecting the coldness in her bones. He had been very civil, very attentive, and even somewhat flirtatious toward her throughout the evening. He had taken a seat beside her in the drawing room after the meal, engaging her in more than one private conversation. Somehow she had managed to behave normally. The evening would have been perfect if not for his unpleasant announcement. *Brighton*. Jane hated the town and she had not even been there.

Three footsteps clicked on the marble floor behind her. "Not to worry, Jane, we shall find you a different match."

Jane turned to face her mother. How could she tell her that she was not interested in a different match? She would wait her entire life for Lord Barnet if she had to. She would not give up unless he married someone else. She couldn't possibly be happy with any other man. But her mother would not understand.

Jane returned her gaze to the window. The stars were invisible, the rain-soaked clouds hiding them from view. But Jane knew they were still there, shining in the sky behind the clouds. Much like the stars, her hope might have been buried and hidden, but she could still feel it burning faintly in her chest.

Chapter 3

Philip Honeyfield, dazed and rather shocked, sat down by the fireplace in his Brighton home. The warmth of the nearby flames spilled over his skin, further increasing the rate of his perspiration. He rubbed his forehead, shaking his head in disbelief.

He, a *marquess*?

Philip couldn't believe the news his solicitor had just revealed to him. The man, small and round, with spectacles to match, had changed Philip's entire life in a matter of seconds. Philip had heard little else aside from the words, read from an official-looking document, 'With the extinction of the title, Duke of Seaford, you, Philip Honeyfield, have hereby been found to be the nearest male descendant of the earlier title, Marquess of Seaford, and must assume the duties of the peerage immediately."

The solicitor had then rambled on about the months of effort that had been taken to find Philip, a distant, multi-great nephew of the late Duke's great grandfather.

Or something of the sort.

Philip combed through his mind, trying to remember the words the solicitor had spoken to him. He had inherited an estate in Seaford, a town just east of Brighton. And he did not want it.

He stared into the fireplace. Yes, Seaford was only a short distance from his childhood town, but it would be a completely different life. He would be a marquess, first of all. He squinted his eyes shut at the thought, unable to believe it was true. He would be wealthy and titled and at a whole new rank in society. He would have spectators watching his every move, his every folly, judging him to be unworthy of his new distinction.

Philip had never imagined his life outside of his home in Brighton. What would happen to his home when he left? Emotion tightened his chest when he thought of the small family he once treasured within those walls. Gone. First his mother then his father, each claimed by the same illness. He had been fourteen years old at the time. He had no siblings, but he had his grandmother, who had sheltered him and raised him from the day his parents died. When Philip had come of age to claim his family's home, he had moved back, haunted by painful memories. This home would always hold those memories, but to leave them behind would be more painful than anything.

His grandmother lived just up the road, on a slight hill facing the ocean. He still visited frequently. In her old age, she could scarcely leave the house unattended, and suffered from loneliness. She was the only family Philip had aside from a few female cousins that visited from Surrey on occasion. In all his life he hadn't the slightest idea that his heritage descended back to the first Marquess of Seaford.

He covered his face with his forearm, grumbling into the sleeve of his jacket. He had witnessed the interactions of titled men here in Brighton. He had seen the ease in which they spoke and acted. Philip did not know a single thing about how to behave as a peer. He had always stood in awe of those men, a bit jealous at the attention they received. Their manner of dress and speech seemed to place them in a different species than the untitled. How could Philip possibly live up to such an expectation?

Philip's stomach flipped at the thought of all the women that would pursue him now, eager to make a match with a marquess. He had little experience where women were concerned. He could not even speak to a woman without tripping over his words and sputtering like a niddicock.

"Ambrose," Philip groaned, calling for his butler. Ambrose had been the butler of Honeyfield Manor for Philip's entire life. He had always been there to offer Philip a listening ear.

Ambrose came to the doorway, his thick, gray eyebrows lifting. "How may I be of assistance?"

Philip crossed his arms, sucking in his cheeks. "It is not a pleasant matter."

"What did your solicitor want with you?" Ambrose entered the room, likely sensing Philip's distress.

"He has informed me that I am the new Marquess of Seaford."

Ambrose's face paled, the deep wrinkles tightening around his eyes. "You? A marquess?"

Philip gave a half-hearted chuckle. If Ambrose didn't

believe Philip could be a suitable marquess then he was definitely hopeless. He released a breath, long and slow, trying to calm the unrest within him. "I will be leaving Honeyfield Manor. I will be master of ... Pengrave, was it? I do not remember." He gave a hard laugh. "How am I to do this?"

Ambrose's face had paled further, and he wrung his hands together. "Will I be losing my position?"

"No, no, of course not! By George, Ambrose! You know I could never employ any other butler. You will have a position with me at Pengrave. I will make sure of it."

The color returned to his butler's face, and his blue eyes flooded with relief. "To be a servant to a marquess ... how extraordinary."

Philip held his head between his hands, the reality of his situation finally reaching his brain. "How can I be a suitable marquess, Ambrose? I will be expected to be gracious and elegant and charming. I do not possess any of those characteristics."

Ambrose nodded, not bothering to flatter Philip with a contradiction. "You are quite right. But surely there is someone who might school you in the matter of peerage."

Philip thought of a man he knew here in Brighton, Lord Ramsbury, soon to be the Earl of Coventry. He frequented the local assembly rooms and was known and admired throughout the entire town, debonair and charming, though his reputation verged on unscrupulous. Even so, society loved him. If Philip could speak to Ramsbury and gather a bit of advice, many of his worries would be put at ease. The man was pompous and arrogant, but very skilled in the art of positive public appearance. Philip needed his help.

"I know just the man," he said.

Philip smiled at the realization that even once Ramsbury assumed his father's title, Philip would still outrank him. His confidence soared at the thought, bringing him to his feet. Before he could lose his resolve, he walked past Ambrose, patting him on the shoulder. Positivity was key to overcoming any hardship, and Philip had endured many. At the front door, he placed his top hat over his dark curls and stepped outside into the cool autumn breeze.

He never thought the day would come that he would seek Lord Ramsbury's advice. Only a desperate situation could bring him to such a decision. But Philip, ungainly and shy, was expected to become a respectable marquess.

And that was a desperate situation indeed.

Chapter 4

Leaves swirled beneath the hooves of Jane's horse as it leapt over a loose branch. Jane flicked the reins, setting her horse at a faster pace as they came out of the trees and onto the wide lawn of the Milton property.

"Faster, Locket," Jane said in a loving voice. The horse continued on, racing across the grass, his hooves skimming the ground as they moved at high speed. Jane laughed, the sound stolen by the wind that whipped at her face and hair.

She threw a brief glance behind her as her horse came to a halt. Jane smiled at her friend Caroline as she emerged from the woods, riding a black mare, who appeared to be behaving uncooperatively once again.

As tradition demanded, Jane took a ride with Caroline each morning, always ending with a race back to the stables. Locket was Jane's horse, and the one Caroline rode, Folly, belonged to Abigail. Abandoned since Abigail's marriage two days before, Folly did not enjoy Caroline's unfamiliar touch.

Jane covered her mouth with a gloved hand, hiding her laughter. Caroline scowled as she approached with Folly. The horse threw its head back in defiance against the pull of the reins. When Caroline saw Jane's laughter, her scowl deepened. Jane straightened the sleeves of her riding habit, trying to appear nonchalant.

"Do you find my suffering humorous?" Caroline asked as she guided her reluctant horse to the stables.

"Only slightly." Jane stifled another laugh as the horse let out an irritated puff of air through its nostrils.

A groom came through the doors of the stables, placing a mounting block at Jane's side and offered his hand. She stepped down from the saddle before crossing the grass to Caroline and Folly.

"I have not told you the dreadful news," she said, looking down at her friend as she dismounted.

Caroline's green eyes widened, all hints of annoyance washed from her face. She pushed back her dark auburn hair as she stepped away from the horse. Jane wished her own hair more closely resembled the color of Caroline's. The red was not so distracting and bright but complemented her other features with subtlety. Jane had met her friend at a house party hosted by Caroline's parents when they were very young, and they had been inseparable ever since.

"What is it?" Caroline asked.

With a long sigh, Jane stroked Folly between the eyes, calming the nervous horse. "It is both dreadful and wonderful at once."

Her friend raised a skeptical eyebrow. "What is the wonderful part?"

"Lord Barnet joined our family for dinner yesterday evening."

Caroline gasped, her eyes rounding into perfect circles. "You cannot be serious! Why did you not tell me this the moment we set out on our ride this morning? You have been speaking of the day you would meet Lord Barnet for years."

Jane nodded solemnly. "As I have. But you have not heard the dreadful part."

Caroline inhaled through her nose, closing her eyes. "I am ready."

"He did not seem entirely opposed to me. He was very attentive, in fact."

Caroline's eyes opened. "That does not sound dreadful."

"I am not finished." Jane felt the despair she had been avoiding creep back into her heart. "He is leaving for Brighton today and will not return until spring."

"Brighton?"

Jane nodded.

"Oh, dear, that *is* quite dreadful," Caroline said in a quiet voice. "But he has chosen a pleasant place to spend the season. Brighton is lovely. My grandmother and cousin live there. I have not visited for several years, but I have a faint memory of the ocean and royal pavilion."

Jane hardly heard her friend's fond description of Brighton. She did not think highly of the place herself. "I daresay I have never received such dreadful news in my life. How can I have a chance to court Lord Barnet if he is in Brighton? He will be stolen by a woman there within a month."

Jane assisted Caroline in bringing Folly back to the

groom who awaited them. With the horses returned to the stables, they walked back toward the house.

Caroline patted Jane on the arm. "Do not lose hope. Perhaps you might find a way to travel to Brighton and pursue him there."

"I cannot appear to be following him, Caroline. That will frighten him away forever. And I doubt my mother would find sufficient reason to accompany me there. My season in London did not meet with success in any sense of the word." Jane shuddered at the memory of London. It had been crowded and extravagant, riddled with the disapproving look in her mother's eyes as Jane hovered near the outskirts of the ballrooms, bored and uninterested in men that did not meet Lord Barnet's standard.

"Perhaps my grandmother would agree to be your chaperone in Brighton. I will write to her today," Caroline said.

Jane's mind raced. She hadn't considered the possibility of following Lord Barnet to Brighton. It was ridiculous. How could she behave with such desperation?

"I still lack a legitimate reason to go to Brighton. I cannot go with the sole intent of chasing Lord Barnet. He will be appalled."

"That is true. You might ... lie? Concoct a story of why you decided to go to Brighton?"

"I cannot lie to my future husband, Caroline. At any rate, my parents will not see the urgency of the situation. Any man of title will please them. But Lord Barnet is the only man I could be happy with." Jane sighed, pressing her hand to her heart. "Why must I be so unfortunate?"

Caroline shrugged. She did not deny that Jane had terrible luck. Fate did not seem to agree with any of her own designs. Perhaps it never would.

When they entered the house, they went straight to the study where Caroline penned a letter to her grandmother in Brighton. It would be days before they received a reply, if one ever came. Caroline had described her grandmother as amiable and pleasant, always showering her grandchildren with affection. Surely she would write Caroline a swift reply. Jane clung to her new hope with eager hands. All she could do was wait.

Lord Barnet had been gone from Ashford nearly a week when Caroline arrived for their morning ride with a letter in hand.

Jane's heart leapt when she saw it—and the enraptured grin on her friend's face.

Caroline hurried across the grass in her emerald green riding habit, waving the letter in the air for Jane to see. Jane pressed down her excitement, reminding herself that Caroline's grandmother's invitation to Brighton would not mean her own parents would allow her to go.

"My grandmother has spoken!" Caroline said, breathless, as she approached. She unfolded the letter, holding it out for Jane to see. "And it is an even more advantageous arrangement than I originally expected."

Jane tore her gaze away from the crooked writing that marked the parchment, her eyes wide. "Please do explain."

"My grandmother is seeking a lady's companion. She has been quite lonely and would like to offer you an allowance and a place to live if you will be her companion."

A lady's companion? Jane bit her lip. It was a respectable position, and she could convince her parents that the allowance she earned would be used to purchase gowns and bonnets and other fashionable items that might aid her in catching the eye of Lord Barnet. The arrangement could very well work in her favor.

Caroline stopped in front of Jane. "As I said before, my grandmother is most agreeable. You will be charged to provide her with conversation and company, as well as attend social gatherings with her. It will be a beneficial arrangement for both of you, I daresay."

The further Jane considered the idea, the more beneficial it began to seem. When she found Lord Barnet there, she could have a feasible reason to explain her presence in Brighton. He would not question it for a moment. She could socialize alongside a respectable companion, Caroline's grandmother, and remain proper in the eyes of society.

Jane's face slowly split into a smile and she clutched her friend's hands. "Hope is not lost!" She laughed, covering her mouth in shock. "I may still have a chance to court Lord Barnet!"

Caroline giggled, jumping in excitement alongside Jane.

"I must speak to my parents immediately." Jane took the letter from Caroline, lifting the skirts of her gray riding habit with one hand, running to the back door of the house. "I will return shortly!" she shouted over her shoulder.

Her legs shook as she entered the house. Her parents would be in the library at this hour, reading the papers before breakfast. She pushed open the heavy wooden doors. As expected, both her parents filled the two leather chairs near the fireplace. Her father glanced up from the paper, his eyes peering over the rims of his spectacles.

"Jane," he greeted with a distracted smile.

"Papa, Mama, I have a proposition for you." She

crossed the room to them, setting the letter in her father's lap. She proceeded to explain the situation, emphasizing the benefits it would bring in her search for a husband.

"Lord Barnet did not seem averse to the idea of courting me. I may further our acquaintance during my time in Brighton." Jane took a deep breath. Her parents stared down at the letter, deep thought evident in the creases of their foreheads. Jane's mother looked up and her lips lifted in a smile.

"Of course, you may go. I do not see any reason to refuse. Your father was just reading something else quite compelling in the *Times*. Should you fail to win Lord Barnet, the nearby town of Seaford has a new marquess. I should like very much to have a daughter married to a marquess." Her eyes sparked with greed. "Can you imagine it? Of all our daughters, Jane making a match with a marquess?"

Her husband chuckled, crossing one leg over his knee. "That would require a true miracle. Our aspirations of a viscount may already be out of reach."

Jane tried to ignore their words as they crashed against her heart like daggers. She hated how much it would please them if she made a titled match.

She also hated how much it would surprise them.

What they didn't realize was that she would still pursue Lord Barnet even if he were a commoner of the simplest sort. She did not care about titles and wealth. She was a genuine romantic.

"How far is Brighton?" her father asked. "A day's journey?" He flipped a page of the *Times*.

"Yes. Only a day, I believe," Jane said.

"We shall accompany you there to see that you are settled. I have always wished to see Brighton but have never found the opportunity." Her father gave a soft smile. "We shall leave next week."

Jane couldn't contain her excitement. She rushed forward and thanked her parents before leaving the room with a spin. Her smile felt impossibly wide as she raced outside to deliver the news to Caroline. She was going to Brighton! She could finally have a real chance at winning Lord Barnet. She sighed as she thought of his deep green eyes, dark, perfect hair, and intense gaze. She could only hope he did not develop an attachment to a different lady before she could arrive.

Caroline received the news with enthusiasm, throwing her arms around Jane. "I am so very happy for you. But I will miss you! Who shall I take my rides with while you are away? I cannot ride here without you."

Jane giggled. "I'm certain Folly will be pleased to be spared your company."

Caroline gasped, shaking a finger at her. "You will return home in the spring to a perfectly trained horse." Her smile grew. "And you will return as Lady Barnet."

Jane's cheeks burned at the thought. Could it be possible? She caught her reflection in the brass button of Caroline's riding habit, her orange hair sticking out at strange angles. Her hope deflated. How could Lord Barnet find her beautiful if her own parents declared her their plainest daughter? As much as she tried to deflect their words, they still made a home in her heart, festering there and filling her with doubt. She stopped herself. She would find a way to finally claim something that her sisters never had. She would finally win. She couldn't let anything ruin her confidence when she arrived in Brighton.

"Tell my grandmother I love her," Caroline said.

Oh, yes. Jane had nearly forgotten that part. She

would have to be a companion to Lady Tabitha, Caroline's grandmother. "I will."

"You must get ready! When do you leave?"

"Next week."

They took their daily ride, discussing all the items Jane would need to purchase before leaving for Brighton, and how she should style her hair at her first ball. Jane's mind spun at the thought that in a week's time she would be beside the ocean, beneath the Brighton sky, and within walking distance of Lord Barnet once again. Her heart soared as she released Locket's reins, savoring the breeze as they raced over the grass.

Chapter 5

Philip sat alone at his long dining table, an abundance of footmen lining the walls of the room. In perfect silence, he ate the meal the skilled cook of Pengrave had prepared for him. His new home, larger than any home he had ever seen, rested on the border between Brighton and Seaford. Pengrave had been the estate of all the late dukes and even the earlier marquesses of the title he now bore.

But those men had each had a family to share it with.

Philip's fork dropped on the ground, clattering in the vast dining room. A footman rushed to pick it up before he could so much as blink, providing him with a new one. Philip sipped from his goblet. He had never felt more awkward within the walls of his own home. But this place, this *Pengrave,* did not feel like home at all.

It had been a fortnight since he had discovered his new role and title. Since that blasted day, the news had been spread throughout the entire country it seemed. He had sought out Lord Ramsbury for advice multiple times, yet Philip still felt more than inadequate.

Ramsbury had told him three things regarding his new status.

He would be noticed. He would be admired. And he would be desired.

Philip had never been any of those things, and he didn't understand how a simple title could alter his entire existence. Philip had spent his life in an opposite manner, always lost behind men like Ramsbury.

But the man's advice could not be ignored. He was acclaimed in all of East Sussex, and Philip needed to discover his secret to success, especially where women were concerned.

Lord Ramsbury could smile at a lady and win her heart, all in an instant. Philip marveled at the skill he possessed. Philip had never given much thought to marriage, always too shy to court the ladies he admired. And he was never admired in return. But as a marquess, Lord Ramsbury had assured him, his fortune would change. Philip didn't like the idea of being desired for his title, but he also didn't like the idea of living in this vast and lonely home for the rest of his life without a family.

His grandmother was all he had. He had only visited her once since he had received his terrible news. Scraping the last of the food from his plate, he stood. He would visit her now. He had little else to occupy his time. He was still in the process of learning how to manage the estate and all the servants there, but he had taken care of such daily tasks that morning. His afternoons were filled with horseback riding, which usually led him back to Brighton where he could visit his friend Adam Claridge and his wife Amelia.

Hurrying out the door, he made his way to the stables. After mounting his horse, he raced westward toward Brighton. On his last visit, his grandmother had told him of her intention to hire a companion, a young woman from Ashford that had been referred by his cousin Caroline. Philip had not known his grandmother to be so lonely and reliant on the assistance of another. Since that moment he had determined to visit her more often.

Thirty minutes later, he dismounted in front of his grandmother's beautiful home. He had spent many years of his life within its walls, and the sight of it now brought a fresh wave of longing. He had not fully appreciated the home before he had moved to Pengrave. His grandmother's home was large and spacious as well, but the interior felt … different. The love and belonging that permeated the walls of her home did not exist in Pengrave. Only cold emptiness.

Philip paused as he noticed a chaise parked in the drive. It seemed his grandmother already had visitors. Perhaps her lady's companion had already arrived from Ashford. He took off his hat, stepping up to the door and giving it a brisk knock.

His grandmother's butler, Mr. Gibbon, let him in, giving him a warm smile of familiarity. Mr. Gibbon's face froze, as if remembering an important detail. "Lord Seaford, it is a pleasure to welcome you."

Philip concealed his grimace. He had not yet grown accustomed to his new form of address. He craned his neck around Mr. Gibbon, an array of voices reaching his ears from the drawing room.

"Mistress Tabitha has received her new companion, Miss Jane Milton, and her parents from Ashford," Mr.

Gibbon said in a quiet voice. "You might join them in the drawing room."

Philip nodded, swallowing his fear. Upon learning of his title, his grandmother's visitors would expect him to act in a certain manner. His lessons from Lord Ramsbury had only just begun.

Pushing open the door to the drawing room, Mr. Gibbon stepped aside, clearing his throat. "The Marquess of Seaford."

All eyes in the room shot to Philip. He saw his grandmother first, sitting in her taupe armchair, her white hair hanging out of her cap, bouncing around her dark eyes. A middle-aged woman sat on the settee beside her, with a thick-bearded man at her side.

Sitting on the armchair nearest to Philip, was a young lady who could only be Miss Jane Milton.

His eyes locked on hers, their pale blue catching him by surprise. Her hair matched the bright orange flames in the hearth, tight curls framing her soft features. While the gazes of her parents held fascination at Philip's entrance, hers held distaste. She looked away fast, focusing on her hands in her lap.

"Philip!" His grandmother's voice, rasped like shards of glass, tore his gaze from the young woman. "Stop standing in the door like a ninny and come greet my guests."

Philip's face grew hot. His grandmother had become less sensitive as she aged, speaking aloud any thought that crossed her mind. She beckoned him over with one finger, the nail of which was extremely long, just like her pointed nose. She had the same brown eyes as Philip, which were the same eyes of his mother. Heavily wrinkled at the corners, his grandmother's eyes sparked with life and laughter, housing memories, both joyful and painful, of the many years she had lived.

Swallowing his embarrassment, Philip stepped into the room with the flourish that Lord Ramsbury had taught him to perfect. He held his chin high, surveying the room with a lazy smile. Philip had been told his ordinary smile was too broad to be showcased by a marquess. He had to show his *superiority*. Trusting Lord Ramsbury's advice, he gave a quick bow to the guests.

"Good day," he said in a shaky voice.

As he lifted his head, his eyes settled on the young woman on the armchair.

"This is Miss Jane Milton," his grandmother said. "She is my new companion."

Miss Milton glanced up from her lap, her long lashes partially concealing her gaze. Philip's stomach flipped. "It is a pleasure to meet you, Miss Milton. My grandmother will be most fortunate to have you in her home." He smiled, surprised that he hadn't made himself sound like a complete bufflehead. Perhaps being a peer had given his confidence the increase it needed.

Miss Milton didn't speak, but simply nodded, looking down at her hands once again. He detected another twinge of annoyance in her brow. He frowned. Lord Ramsbury had promised that women would flock to him with his new title. This young woman appeared vexed by his very existence.

"Sit, my boy. You need not appear so lost." His grandmother turned to Mrs. Milton. "As you know, Philip is my grandson. I had not an inkling that his father's line contained sufficient relation to bring a marquess to our family. As an orphan at the age of fourteen he came to live in this very home with me." She proceeded to begin telling the group of the many years he lived in her home, and the many misfortunes that had befallen him. Philip walked to the armchair beside Miss Milton, sitting down before he could lose his nerve.

"Lord Seaford, how have you managed to overcome such unfortunate circumstances?" Mr. Milton asked from across the room, one hand rubbing his bearded chin.

Philip felt the weight of several gazes on his face, in particular the icy blue gaze of Miss Milton beside him. He let the question rest in his mind for a long moment, the answer unclear. With the expectation of providing the perfect answer weighing over him, he couldn't think clearly. How would a marquess respond? As Mr. Philip Honeyfield he could have spoken with ease, but he felt as if he had taken on a new identity, one that was expected to perform with perfection. He took a deep breath. "I could not have survived without the goodness of my grandmother. I owe her an immense debt of gratitude."

Mr. Milton nodded in heartfelt understanding. "Do you enjoy your Pengrave residence?"

Philip started to nod but changed his mind. He could not lie. "It is a beautiful and very… spacious home. But I must admit it is quite lonely."

Mr. and Mrs. Milton exchanged a quick glance, a smile touching Mrs. Milton's lips as her eyes slid from Philip to her daughter.

His ears burned. He had not meant to suggest that he was seeking a wife, but it seemed his words had delivered that message on their own. He glanced at Miss Milton in the chair beside him, the centers of her cheeks turning an endearing pink as she looked a warning at her mother.

"I hope you will find a way to remedy that situation, Lord Seaford," her mother said with a demure smile. As if remembering something very important, she gasped.

"Jane, perhaps you might sing the song you have been practicing."

Philip took the opportunity to watch her again. Miss Milton was uncommonly pretty, a unique beauty to her features. His heart flipped in his chest like a dry fish as her eyes flicked to his. She tucked a wayward strand of hair behind her ear, obviously uncomfortable with her mother's proposed idea. She remained silent.

"Come now, Jane, the marquess would surely love to hear a song." Her father met Philip's eyes, asking for encouragement.

Philip didn't know what to say. Miss Milton would probably hate him for requesting that she sing, but to deny her father's words would be extremely rude. He wished he could save her from the performance she seemed to dread, but propriety forced his hand. And, after all, her father was right. Philip did want to hear her sing.

"Indeed." He turned in his chair toward Miss Milton. "I imagine you have a voice. Er—I mean—a *lovely* voice." He cringed at his own words.

Her lips pressed together as she dared a look at him, a light scowl marking her forehead. He sat back. What had he done to deserve a scowl like that? Contrary to Ramsbury's counsel, Philip cast her a wide smile of encouragement, hoping to dispel the annoyance that flickered in her gaze.

She looked away, shifting uncomfortably under the attention of the room. "Very well," she said in a soft voice. Standing up, she threw one more glance at Philip before venturing to the pianoforte.

Her mother stood. "I shall accompany you."

Philip studied Miss Milton as she and her mother prepared for her song. He had never seen hair with such a strong color appear so beautiful. The blue of her eyes complemented the red tones of her hair, and her shy disposition was so endearing Philip could hardly look away. This woman was to be his grandmother's companion? Here was another reason to visit often.

Mrs. Milton played the first note on the pianoforte, progressing a slow melody in introduction. Philip sat forward in his chair, waiting for Miss Milton's voice.

The first words escaped her mouth, flooding his ears with a clear and beautiful soprano. He listened in awe as she sang to the haunting melody. She swayed slightly to the music, as if the words and notes had become embedded within her, spreading out through her body. She met Philip's eyes only once, but it was he who looked away, embarrassed by the admiration that surely showed in his gaze.

When the last note rang in the air, he threw his hands together in applause. The room joined, but with only half the enthusiasm as Philip. Miss Milton's cheeks reddened, and a hint of a smile touched her lips. Philip's heart skipped. He wondered how she would look with a real smile.

She reclaimed her seat beside him, crossing her hands in her lap. He smiled, hoping to draw her eyes to him.

It didn't work.

"Did you enjoy the performance, Lord Seaford?" Mr. Milton asked him.

Philip could hardly grasp his own thoughts. His mind and heart were still reeling from the beauty of the song and Miss Milton. "I enjoyed it very much. Rarely do I have the honor of hearing a voice as beautiful as your daughter's."

Miss Milton's head turned at his words, and he caught her gaze for a brief moment before she looked away. He swallowed, forcing himself to have the courage to speak directly to her.

"You have a true talent."

She touched her hair, shifting in her chair. "Thank you, Lord Seaford."

Being addressed as *Lord Seaford* grated on him. When he had been simply Mr. Honeyfield, people had not felt the need to tread so carefully around him. Every interaction he had experienced since he became a marquess had felt very forced.

"Truly, I am in earnest," he said. "You should never hesitate to sing for an audience."

Miss Milton thanked him with her eyes, and his breath caught in his throat. He had never been at ease around pretty young women, but something about this one was different. He had never been struck so instantly by the desire to come to know another person. She was hiding behind a shy facade, and he wanted to draw a smile and a prolonged conversation from her.

"I sound rather like a horse when I sing," he said. "It is not a sound you wish to hear, I assure you."

Polite laughter from her parents reached his ears, but not even a smile broke Miss Milton's stoic expression. She simply looked at him in masked curiosity. He cleared his throat.

"Do you ride, Miss Milton?"

"I do. I have a horse in Ashford. His name is Locket." Half her mouth lifted in a smile and her expression turned wistful. "I wish I could have brought him with me."

Philip grinned in victory. He had struck a topic she wished to speak more than one word about. "My estate is equipped with many horses. Perhaps you could . . . accompany my grandmother there for a ride."

Before she could respond, her mother gasped. "Oh, my daughter would like that very much."

Another twinge of annoyance bit Miss Milton's brow, but she smoothed her expression with a shrug. "I suppose."

Philip's heart sank. She did not seem at all inclined to spend time at his estate. In fact, she seemed repulsed by it. He should not have expected that a title would change his luck with women in an instant. He had grown accustomed to rejection as Philip Honeyfield but had not expected it as Lord Seaford. How did Lord Ramsbury manage to be so successful? It puzzled Philip to no end.

"You are all welcome at Pengrave at any time," he said, sweeping his hand around the room.

Mrs. Milton sighed in dramatic regret. "If only Mr. Milton and I were staying in Brighton long enough to visit. We depart in two days. But I am pleased to know my daughter is welcome."

Philip nodded. He couldn't help but glance at Miss Milton again. She avoided his eyes, reverting to her first tactic of staring at her hands.

Philip's grandmother clapped, shifting forward. "Miss Milton is accompanying me to a ball held at Clemsworth tomorrow evening. You must attend, Philip."

Philip had already received his invitation. Clemsworth was the residence of Lord Ramsbury and his father, the Earl of Coventry. He dreaded going. It would be his first private assembly as a marquess, and he did not want to make a fool of himself. But Miss Milton would be there. The thought of asking her for a dance twisted his insides in knots.

"I will be there," he said, forcing a smile.

His grandmother gave him a nod of approval, settling

back into the cushions of her chair. "It is not every day that your grandson becomes a marquess. I must take every opportunity to be seen with you in public." She winked at him.

He gave a loud laugh. He stopped himself when all eyes in the room looked his way. *Blast it.* He had been performing well until that point. He turned his laughter into a cough, straightening his posture. "You will likely receive more embarrassment than praise to be seen with me, grandmother."

She clicked her tongue. "Nonsense."

Philip spent the next hour in the drawing room, discussing everything from politics to travel and weather. He managed to pull only a few brief comments out of Miss Milton, and he caught the disapproving stare that her mother cast her each time she snubbed him.

He didn't understand it, but he found Miss Milton to be fascinating, despite her quiet personality. He suspected there was much more to her character that she was choosing to hide from him. When he took his leave, he threw her one last smile.

In response she gave nothing but a curt nod.

Frustration rose within him as he walked outside and mounted his horse. He had a new destination in mind; he was not returning to Pengrave immediately. He would pay Lord Ramsbury a visit while he was in Brighton. With the ball approaching the next evening, and a woman he wanted to impress, he needed all the advice he could get. Philip knew he was likely to find Lord Ramsbury in the assembly rooms of town, so he set off in that direction.

As he thought about his behavior in his grandmother's drawing room, he decided he had performed fairly well. He had made polite conversation, avoided boisterous laughter, and had only made a fool of himself once or twice. Lord Ramsbury would be proud of him.

Perhaps Philip wasn't entirely helpless after all.

Chapter 6

Jane watched out the front window as Lord Seaford and his horse grew smaller in the distance. Caroline had not mentioned that her cousin was the new Marquess of Seaford.

She ought to have warned her.

Turning to face her parents, Jane was not surprised to find two disapproving stares. Lady Tabitha, Caroline's grandmother, watched her grandson's retreat as well, but with a loving smile lifting her wrinkled cheeks.

"What an agreeable man your grandson is, Lady Tabitha," Jane's mother said before casting Jane a look of censure.

"Oh, yes. There are few men equal to his honorable character." Lady Tabitha smiled warmly before lifting her gaze from the window.

Jane's mother wrapped her finger around a curl in her

hair, as if trying to appear less interested than she truly was. "Does he visit here often?"

"As often as he is able. He has become a busy man. Managing an estate the size of Pengrave is not a simple task."

"As I would imagine."

Jane moved her gaze to the window once again, disinterested in the conversation of Lord Seaford. Why must he have come here? She knew her parents would never surrender in their efforts to match her with him now. Lord Barnet would appear to be insignificant compared to a marquess. Viscounts were ranked below both marquesses and earls. Jane's parents already had two daughters married to *earls*. The idea was becoming a bore to them. They desired more honor than that.

Jane was appalled at the obvious effort her mother had made to showcase her talents to Lord Seaford. Asking Jane to sing was a tactic her mother hadn't used for years, never wanting to steal attention from her other three daughters when eligible gentlemen came to call.

Jane often wondered how her parents would react if she did not marry at all. Would she reach an age when they would finally relent? Once their hope in her securing a good match was lost, would they even love her? The idea brought a lump to her throat.

Jane swallowed, focusing her gaze on the distant ocean. She had arrived in Brighton just that morning and hadn't yet had the opportunity to explore the coast and town center. Caroline had told her that the assembly rooms were always filled with tourists and young people looking to socialize. She suspected those rooms were where Lord Barnet resided at that very moment.

*Lord Barne*t. She longed to see him again. A small sigh escaped her as she gazed out the window.

"Are you already pining for my grandson?" Lady Tabitha asked, a smile in her voice.

Jane jerked her eyes from the window, shaking her head with a laugh. "No, I was simply thinking of the beauty of Brighton."

"It's a lovely town, is it not? I shall never leave." Lady Tabitha gave a wide grin that reminded Jane of the one Lord Seaford had flaunted. Jane had not known how to react to such a smile directed at her from a man. She hadn't known what to do with the attention. Men of wealth and title had never paid her any notice before. A small part of her burned with guilt over snubbing him, but she did not have any other choice. If she meant to convey the message to her parents that she did not wish to pursue him, she had to do it.

Jane's father stood, recalling her attention. "Your mother and I hope to explore the town before we depart and see the shops."

A surge of excitement entered Jane's heart before she realized that she would not be accompanying them. She was a lady's companion now.

Jane's mother turned to Lady Tabitha. "May we borrow our daughter for a moment outside before we depart?"

"Certainly." The old woman gave a pleasant smile, ushering them toward the door with her hand.

The dreaded look of censure entered Jane's father's expression as he motioned with his eyes for her to stand. She sighed inwardly, pushing herself to her feet. Her mother placed one hand on Jane's back as she ushered her out the front door of the house. Jane's eyes adjusted to the bright sunlight, the sound of various birds mingling with the distant ocean spray.

Her mother turned to her, a controlled scowl pinching her face. Her blue eyes burned with suppressed anger. "How dare you snub Lord Seaford?"

Jane willed herself not to become defensive. "I did not find him agreeable."

"Not agreeable? I daresay he did not find *you* to be agreeable at all. What with your frowning and—and . . . ignoring."

"I don't care, Mama." The more her parents wanted her to pursue Lord Seaford, the more opposed to the idea Jane became. It was not her dream to be matched with a marquess. It was only her dream to marry the man she adored, and his name was none other than Lord Barnet. She could not settle for a match with any other man when there was still hope for him.

Jane's nonchalance fed the flame of anger in her mother's eyes. "We did not bring you to Brighton for you to toss this opportunity to the wind because you *do not care*."

"You brought me to Brighton to pursue Lord Barnet."

Her mother lifted her chin. "And pursue him you shall. But you must keep Lord Seaford as an available option. It is likely that Lord Barnet will find a much more suitable bride. Lord Seaford expressed more interest in you than Lord Barnet by far. Do not lose your chance."

Jane's heart dropped, hot tears burning behind her eyes. She refused to give up hope on Lord Barnet, no matter what her mother said. She cursed Lord Seaford in her mind. Had he truly seemed interested in her? Jane had been too focused on avoiding him to notice. But it did not matter because she was not interested in *him*.

Jane kept her mouth closed. She couldn't verbally agree to her mother's request. In truth, she hoped she never saw Lord Seaford again.

Her father whispered in her mother's ear, calming the

anger in her eyes by small increments. Jane wished she were free to venture away from Lady Tabitha's house and find Lord Barnet at the assembly rooms, or see the ocean, or peruse the shops in town, but she could not do so alone. And she certainly didn't want to accompany her parents at this moment.

It had just begun, and her trip to Brighton already felt like it had been ruined. She took a deep and steadying breath. At least when her parents returned to Ashford she could enjoy more freedom.

Jane looked up at the sky. The area above her stirred with white and charcoal, brewing a rain storm.

"We will return shortly," her father said, following her gaze to the sky. "Our exploration will not be long if we encounter a storm. Go inside now and tend to Lady Tabitha."

Jane's mother took her husband's arm before offering a pitiful frown. "Your position as Lady Tabitha's companion might have been unwise. How many social events will she be willing to venture to? Very few. I expect your opportunities to see Lord Barnet will be few as well. But with Lord Seaford visiting his grandmother so often, you will have the perfect chance to win him. Do not forget it."

Jane didn't try to protest. The weighted reality of her mother's words struck her, and she felt as if she were sinking into the path on which she stood. With one more glance at the churning sky, Jane ducked her head and hurried back to the house, escaping without a single drop of rain touching her hair. She loved rain, but not the effect it had on her hair.

Leaning against the door, she breathed out the myriad of emotions that constricted her heart. She did not have time to sort through them. She would not waste another moment in Brighton that could cost her the prize she had come for. As she imagined failure, finding herself as a lonely lady's companion for the remaining autumn and winter months, witnessing another woman on Lord Barnet's arm, Jane found renewed determination.

"Lady Tabitha," she said as she entered the drawing room, "how do you wish to spend the afternoon?"

Lady Tabitha glanced up from the book she had been holding, her spectacles sliding down her long nose. "Caroline claimed you were one of invigorating conversation." She patted the arm of the chair beside her. "You might sit down so we may get to know one another."

That was not the answer Jane was hoping for. Containing her disappointment, she crossed the room and sat beside Lady Tabitha. "My conversation is not that invigorating, I assure you."

"Was I wrong to offer you the position?" Lady Tabitha asked, tipping her head to one side.

"Not at all. I only wondered if you would rather explore the town. I have heard the assembly rooms are invigorating as well."

Lady Tabitha raised one pale eyebrow, a smirk twisting her mouth. "I frequented those rooms often in my younger days. In fact—"

"Would you like to go today?"

Lady Tabitha pursed her lips at Jane's interruption. "I would prefer to remain home until the ball at Clemsworth."

Jane crossed her arms, biting back her annoyance. "Very well."

Lady Tabitha watched her, the deep brown of her eyes permeating Jane's very soul. A glint of humor entered her gaze. "Caroline indicated that there was a man you were pursuing here in Brighton."

Jane's eyes widened. Her cheeks warmed. "Did she?"

"Indeed."

Jane interlaced her fingers, watching her thumbs as they spun around each other. "Is that all she said?"

"Not so." Lady Tabitha's eyes sparked with mischief. "Do I appear helpless and lonely to you?"

Jane looked up. When she had first seen Lady Tabitha that morning, her first thought had been that the woman was quite friendly and loud for one so elderly and experienced in social propriety. She spoke of the many visitors she received in her home each week. Jane had found it rather strange that Lady Tabitha had sought a lady's companion at all.

"You do not," Jane answered, her voice hesitant.

"Precisely."

"What?"

She threw out her hand. "I never desired a companion, child. Caroline expressed to me the nature of your dilemma, and I decided to assist you in getting to Brighton." Lady Tabitha grinned, throwing a wink at Jane.

Her jaw dropped.

"I have sufficient funds to give you an allowance, of course, but I will be lenient in my requirements of you. If there is a social event in which you might find this Lord Barnet, I will be pleased to be your escort."

Jane couldn't believe what she was hearing. Caroline *and* her grandmother had been conspiring to match Jane with Lord Barnet? She liked Lady Tabitha much more already. "Are you quite serious?"

"I am always serious when the matter concerns handsome gentlemen." The old woman winked again.

Jane laughed, and it came out much louder than she intended. She covered her mouth. Lady Tabitha chuckled, leaning forward in her chair. "Well, shall we go to the assembly rooms?"

"I thought you wished to stay home until the ball?" Jane said.

"Posh. I may be old but I am not boring. I shall not surpass an opportunity to mingle with my favorite acquaintances."

Jane's stomach lurched with sudden terror. What if Lord Barnet was indeed there? What would she say to him? She had rehearsed the words in her mind countless times, but in the moment they were sure to come out wrong. She tried to answer Lady Tabitha, but her throat was too dry.

The old woman stood, eyeing Jane with a furrowed brow. "Come, Miss Milton. Or have you changed your mind?"

Jane shook her head hard, forcing her legs not to shake as she stood up. "I am simply… surprised. That is all."

Lady Tabitha threw her a look of suspicion, but it slowly transformed into a smile. "Are you afraid of Lord Barnet?"

"No!" Jane corrected her defensive tone. "No, I am not."

Shuffling across the room, Lady Tabitha chuckled under her breath. "You sound very much like Philip."

"Who?" Jane followed Lady Tabitha to the door of the drawing room, passing a pair of footmen in the entry hall.

"My grandson, Lord Seaford."

Jane rolled her eyes when Lady Tabitha turned around. She was growing tired of hearing about Lord Seaford. Fortunately, with Lady Tabitha's assistance in her pursuit of Lord Barnet, Jane would be able to avoid the house when Lord Seaford came to visit. She could write to her parents and explain that he simply was not interested in her. She would never have to see him if she didn't wish to.

Within minutes a coach was prepared to convey them to the assembly rooms in town. Jane secured the ribbons of her pale blue bonnet under her chin. Lady Tabitha wore an extravagant turban, complete with two exotic feathers. They sat across one another in the coach, and Jane couldn't help but notice the intent stare Lady Tabitha had fixed her with. Jane focused her attention out the window at the passing ocean, but she felt Lady Tabitha's stare burning on her cheek.

"The ocean is beautiful," Jane said, uncomfortable with the old woman's intent study. She stared at the gentle waves as they rose and fell.

"Is it as beautiful as Lord Barnet?"

Jane's eyes shot to Lady Tabitha, who gave a hoot of laughter.

"Come now, is it?"

Jane could scarcely believe such a question had been directed at her. Her hands grew slick with perspiration. She gave an awkward laugh. "Both possess a unique beauty. How can I compare the two? The only commonality between the ocean and Lord Barnet is the color of his eyes. They are not entirely blue, but rather green, like the deepest area of a lake, or the sea beneath a stormy sky."

"How charming."

Jane nodded, her cheeks warming.

"Tell me more of this Lord Barnet. How long have you been his acquaintance?"

Jane had been dreading that question. Since the first day she had *seen* him, it had been seven years. Since the first day she had been *introduced* to him, little more than seven days. "Oh, he has been in my heart for many years," Jane said.

"But when did you first meet him?"

Jane squirmed under the watchful gaze of Lady Tabitha. How embarrassing it would be to tell her that she had only recently met Lord Barnet. But Jane had never been one to countenance the act of lying. As a child she had been caught in many lies, always chewing her lip or wringing her hands in an attempt to hide them. Now Jane claimed honesty as one of her strongest virtues. But situations could arise that demanded a small lie.

"I cannot remember, for it has been a very long time," she said before dropping her gaze.

"I see." Lady Tabitha's gruff voice did not sound entirely convinced.

Jane fixed her eyes on the window. Her heart flipped and fluttered in her chest like a caged thing as she rehearsed in her mind what she would say to Lord Barnet. It was easy when she was practicing with herself, but to do it with a set of ocean-green eyes looking into hers would be a different matter.

When the carriage came to a halt, Jane and Lady Tabitha were helped down by the coachman. Lady Tabitha, spry as she was for her age, led the way into the main entrance of the first level. Jane examined her surroundings, feeling her confidence shrink with each step.

There were dozens of well-dressed, elegant and beautiful young women and men engaged in conversation within the brightly lit room. It was the ballroom area, and Jane could see the door to a smaller card room to the far left of the space. Her heart raced as she discreetly scanned the room for Lord Barnet. He could not be easily missed.

As she cast her eyes around the room, she caught sight

of a familiar face. Lord Seaford stood against the adjacent wall, staring directly at her. *What the devil is he doing here?* Jane thought, annoyance tightening in her chest. A man stood beside him, the appearance of wealth and title evident in the smirk of his face.

Lady Tabitha gasped. "Oh, Philip is here! How coincidental." She chuckled, wagging her finger at him as she approached. Jane lagged behind, unwilling to appear eager to see him. She had seen him not an hour before. Could she not avoid him for longer than that? She glanced over her shoulder, desperately searching for Lord Barnet one last time among the crowd. She did not see him. Disappointment dropped in her stomach like a heavy stone.

Lady Tabitha reached Lord Seaford. She looked so small beside him. Lord Seaford was tall, and the man beside him possessed the same trait. Lord Seaford smiled down at his grandmother before his eyes found Jane once again. A slight red tinted his face as he cast her a broad smile.

Jane had been impressed with his ability to put forth a friendly demeanor among strangers. She had never met a man with such an ever-present smile.

"Miss Milton," Lord Seaford's cheeks deepened in color yet again. He cleared his throat, his smile not lessening in the slightest. "It has been ages since I last saw you."

Jane gave a half-smile, her eyes wandering the room for Lord Barnet.

"Is this your first visit to the assembly rooms?"

It took her a moment to realize Lord Seaford was still addressing her. Her eyes flew up to his. He tilted his head to the side in curiosity, his brown eyes wide. There was something youthful and endearing about his face, but it lacked the mysterious, dark, brooding quality of Lord

Barnet. Even if Lord Seaford were interested in her, she could never court him. It would please her parents too much.

"Indeed," she replied.

"How do you find them?"

"Quite … crowded."

Lord Seaford smiled again, and Jane smiled back before remembering that she should not be encouraging him. She corrected her expression, looking at the ground.

"I traveled the continent early this year. I believe the Brighton assembly rooms to hold the most admirable of people in all of Europe." His voice came out quick, as if he were trying to keep her attention.

Jane glanced up only to acknowledge that she had heard him. The man that stood next to Lord Seaford stepped forward, a definite saunter in his step. His handsome features were clouded by the pompous smile he wore. Lord Seaford introduced the man to Jane as Lord Ramsbury, the eldest son of the Earl of Coventry.

After offering Jane a short greeting, Lord Ramsbury engaged Lady Tabitha in conversation. His sharp blue eyes flicked toward Jane as he tapped Lord Seaford's arm. Lord Seaford stumbled closer to Jane, stopping directly in front of her. "Have you traveled to any fascinating places, Miss Milton?"

She inched back a step, unsettled by his closeness. "Only Brighton. I have never been outside of England, and never to the coast." She surveyed the room, avoiding Lord Seaford's chestnut brown eyes as they stared expectantly at hers.

"At least you have now seen the ocean. It is beautiful, is it not?"

"Quite."

Lord Seaford was silent for a long moment, before blurting, "Miss Milton."

She met his eyes, taken aback by the intensity of his gaze. "I wish to invite you to come riding with me at my estate on the morrow."

Jane froze. Since she had come out in society she had never been extended such an invitation from a man. She had been dreaming of this moment for years, but with one alteration: that the invitation *not* come from Lord Seaford. Many women would consider themselves very fortunate to be invited to go riding with a marquess, but she did not want to at all. Without realizing it, she released a sigh of discontent.

The hopeful expression of Lord Seaford dropped, and he stammered, "Of course my grandmother would accompany you. She is in need of fresh air, to be sure."

Jane pressed her lips together before forcing herself to nod. To refuse would be far too rude, and she had been rude enough already. Guilt twisted in her stomach as Lord Seaford's mouth widened in a smile.

"If you will extend the invitation to my grandmother, I would be most grateful."

Jane nodded again, afraid to speak, as if a simple word would be mistaken as encouragement. She had never dealt with the challenge of detaining a man's interest in her. Behind Lord Seaford's shoulder, Jane saw Lord Ramsbury watching their exchange, only half-listening to Lady Tabitha.

"Seaford." Lord Ramsbury stepped forward, placing his hand on his friend's shoulder. "Let us finish our game of chess in the card room and leave these charming ladies to socialize."

Lord Seaford did not seem inclined to leave, raising

one eyebrow at his friend before turning his smile on Jane once again. "I will send my carriage in the morning to convey you and Lady Tabitha to my estate."

Before Jane could offer her reply, Lord Ramsbury gave a pained smile, pulling Lord Seaford by the arm in the direction of the card room. Lady Tabitha grinned at their retreating forms, clicking her tongue. "My Philip is smitten with you, I'm afraid. If he continues with his attention in public, he will be honor bound to marry you."

Jane's heart lurched. "But I am not interested in marrying him." Jane remembered that she was speaking to his grandmother. The woman wouldn't appreciate Jane's aversion to marrying her beloved grandson. "Of course, he is an amiable man, but my heart belongs to Lord Barnet."

"Of course." Lady Tabitha nodded in understanding. "But would you consider Lord Ramsbury? He is *very* handsome."

Jane shook her head. It wouldn't surprise her if the man spent hours each day in front of a looking glass, practicing his pompous smirk and charming smiles. Even his clothing dripped with arrogance, just as did his every motion.

With a sigh, Jane remembered Lord Seaford's request. "Your grandson has invited us to go riding on the morrow. He was certain you would be willing to travel there."

"Oh? He has invited you to ride?" A hint of disapproval marked her brow. "You mustn't encourage him if you have your heart set on another man. I will not have you breaking my grandson's heart."

"I have not encouraged him, I assure you. I have tried to do the opposite."

Lady Tabitha tsked, adjusting the feather in her turban. "I suspect a romantic like Philip would not require encouragement to lose his heart. The poor boy."

Guilt writhed in Jane's stomach once again. What would her parents think if they knew the Marquess of Seaford was pursuing her and she was deflecting every advance?

They would have her head, she was sure of it.

Chapter 7

"You invited her to come riding . . . with your *grandmother?*" Edward Beaumont, Lord Ramsbury, threw his head back in a burst of laughter.

Philip scowled. "What's wrong with that? She's her companion!"

"You cannot expect to romance her with your grandmother sitting on the back end of her horse." Lord Ramsbury shook his head at the chessboard that sat between them.

Philip ran his hand through his hair, sitting back with a huffed breath. "I don't possess your skill."

"My skill is and forever will be unmatched," Lord Ramsbury said, half his mouth lifting in a smirk as he moved his chess piece. "Unmatched by all except Adam Claridge." His sharp blue eyes dug into Philip's as he glanced up, and his jaw tightened when he studied the board again.

Adam Claridge was among Philip's closest friends. They had been friends since childhood, as they had both grown up in Brighton and attended boarding school together. Just that summer, Adam had married Miss Amelia Buxton, a woman whom Lord Ramsbury had been pursuing. Until Philip had started meeting with Lord Ramsbury for advice, he hadn't realized the extent of the man's feelings toward her.

Lord Ramsbury had been left bitter and heartbroken to say the least.

"I should have put forth greater effort to win her heart." Lord Ramsbury said, speaking more to the piece he held than to Philip. "I suppose I wasn't used to making an effort for attention. I should have asked her to marry me again. I should have . . . kissed her."

Philip's eyes widened. "Kissed her?"

Lord Ramsbury looked up, amusement flickering over his features. "Have you never kissed a woman, Seaford?"

Philip crossed one leg over his knee, feigning intense interest in the chess game. "Of course, I have."

Lord Ramsbury shook his head, pointing an accusing finger at Philip. "You haven't!"

"I have!"

"You have not. You are an awful liar."

Philip hated confessing such an embarrassing thing to Lord Ramsbury, who had certainly charmed more than one secret kiss out of an array of unsuspecting women. Philip kept his mouth shut, refusing to admit his shortcoming verbally.

"You must remedy that situation as soon as possible," Lord Ramsbury said with a chuckle. "I will not deem you a rightful man if you do not. And certainly not a marquess."

Philip scoffed. "I'm not fond of the idea of risking an innocent woman's reputation."

"That is why you must seek her company alone, with no grandmothers lurking about." Lord Ramsbury snorted into laughter.

"I am not going to kiss Miss Milton." Philip shook his head. The idea was preposterous. He hardly knew her, and she had been aloof toward him yet again. He was certainly not going to kiss a woman that he knew didn't *want* to be kissed by him.

Lord Ramsbury shrugged. "Then someone else will."

Philip grumbled to himself, the chessboard becoming blurred as he stared at it. He did not particularly like the idea of another man sweeping Miss Milton off her feet, discovering her true character, coercing a smile from her pretty face. He hardly knew her, yes, but he could not give up the opportunity to come to know her. Still, that did not mean he had to *kiss* her. Lord Ramsbury was mad.

Philip clamped his hands together before looking up at his new friend. "I do not wish to establish myself as a rake. That is all kissing Miss Milton would accomplish. In truth, I could hardly *speak* to her today without acting like a simpleton."

Lord Ramsbury rolled his eyes. "You ask for my help in making you a proper marquess, yet you refuse my advice."

"Because your advice is absurd!" Philip laughed. "Do you truly believe Miss Amelia Buxton's heart would have changed with a brief kiss?"

"It would not have been a *brief* kiss, I assure you," he grumbled.

Philip chuckled, shaking his head. "I suspect Miss Buxton would have made certain it was more brief than you would have liked."

With a scowl, Lord Ramsbury looked down at the board. As much as it pleased Philip to see a wealthy man like Lord Ramsbury lose to a man like Adam Claridge, he still hated to see the pain in his new friend's eyes. Although Lord Ramsbury pretended in public to be unphased by his rejection, Philip could see that it had cut him all the way to his core. His heart had been thoroughly affected, not just his pride.

Philip softened his voice. "I'm sorry, Edward. I will likely face a rejection soon as well."

He looked up, hard and fast. "You will not. As my pupil, you must obey me, and I demand that you avoid rejection. Failure is not an option!"

Philip raised his hands in defense, unsettled by the fire in Lord Ramsbury's eyes. "Very well."

Lord Ramsbury sat back, crossing his arms in a sudden calm. "How are you going to do it?"

"Do what?"

"Kiss her."

"I never agreed to that!"

Lord Ramsbury let out a sigh of exasperation, raking his hand through his dark blond hair. "You are the most stubborn pupil I have ever encountered. Think of the consequences."

"Yes, that is precisely why I refuse to do it. Miss Milton's reputation could be grievously hurt."

"Think of the *positive* consequences. If you kiss her properly, away from the watchful eye of society, you will have become a real marquess, and a real man. You will have pleased your instructor," he pointed a finger at himself, "and you will have communicated to Miss Milton in the most concise way of your affection."

Lord Ramsbury made a tempting argument. Philip stopped himself, shaking his head so firmly his neck cracked. He rubbed the back of it as he stood. "No. No, I will not. Good day, Ramsbury."

"Seaford!" Lord Ramsbury laughed as Philip hurried out the door. In the ballroom, he caught sight of Miss Milton, still standing beside his grandmother, surveying the crowd with a look of dejection.

She was not easy to miss among the throng with her bright hair and pale eyes. Why was she so fascinating to him? All she had done was snub him and frown at the ground, yet he could not remove her from his mind since he had first seen her just hours before. Was Ramsbury right? Could he win her favor? Before he could do that, he would need to uncover her true nature. If she was truly his cousin Caroline's dearest friend, then she could not be as severe as she pretended to be.

Would he kiss her? No. But had Lord Ramsbury's advice been beneficial in the past? Yes.

This piece of advice, however, was far outside Philip's bounds—and his capability. He was too much a coward.

Mounting his horse, he set off for Pengrave. Nervousness choked him as he thought of the next morning when Miss Milton would come to his estate. Would she be impressed? He now possessed more influence than the common gentleman when it came to property and wealth. But it was not his property that he would need to impress Miss Milton, it was himself.

And that was the greatest challenge he had ever faced.

Chapter 8

Lady Tabitha had been gracious enough to have a room prepared for Jane's parents when they returned that night. Jane had avoided telling them about her second encounter with Lord Seaford, but Lady Tabitha had spilled the news.

The rapture that followed from Jane's mother had been too much to bear. Mrs. Milton had always been skilled at containing her excitement when propriety dictated so, but the news of Jane's upcoming ride with Lord Seaford had been an exception to that practice.

Jane sat on the edge of her bed the next morning, rubbing the sleep from her eyes. As if her mother had sensed that Jane had awoken, the door to her bedchamber cracked open. Her mother stepped into the room, a wicked grin on her lips. "I am very excited."

"I did not doubt it," Jane said.

"My daughter, a potential marchioness." Her mother gave a squeal, closing the door behind her as she rushed in. She wore a dark blue gown, her hair already styled in a neat twist. "You must not lose Lord Seaford's favor, Jane. There are many women here in Brighton, so you must keep his attention on you. I have chosen your emerald green riding habit, as it compliments your hair. Suzanne is here to style it for you."

Her maid, Suzanne, had accompanied Jane and her parents to Brighton. Much to Jane's relief, her mother had told her that Suzanne would be staying there with Jane for the extent of her trip. Jane relied heavily on her maid's skill to make her hair presentable.

At the sound of her name, Suzanne opened the door, offering Jane a smile and a curtsy. Jane had welcomed the effort to make her beautiful when it had been to impress Lord Barnet, but with only Lord Seaford to impress, Jane was not motivated in the slightest. But the ball that night would be a different matter. Her heart surged with excitement and fear. It would be her first opportunity to impress Lord Barnet in Brighton. With her parents no longer fully endorsing the pursuit, she would need to use her own skill and confidence to capture his attention.

When her hair was styled and she was dressed in her green riding habit, her mother ushered her down the stairs and to the front entrance where Lord Seaford's carriage awaited her and Lady Tabitha. For Lady Tabitha's sake, Jane smiled. There was little from this excursion that would benefit Jane, but she looked at the situation in a positive light. At least she would get to ride a horse.

The drive to Pengrave would take at least a full hour by coach, so Jane took the opportunity to study the scenery of Brighton from the window of the carriage. The royal pavilion, framed in blue sky and sea, grew smaller in the distance as they traveled.

As her position required, Jane conversed with Lady Tabitha without appearing bored, which she was quite proud of. After what felt like an eternity, Lady Tabitha's eyes widened, and she pointed one of her long fingernails toward the window. "Pengrave."

Jane turned, her jaw dropping at the estate that loomed ahead. To its credit, Pengrave was the largest estate Jane had ever seen. Constructed of dark gray stone, it captured the essence of the dim morning sky. The property was covered with neat grass and lush green bushes and trees, the tops of which were just beginning to adopt the colors of autumn. Jane could only imagine how many rooms the estate had, and how many servants were required to maintain such an extensive property.

"My grandson has much to look after." Lady Tabitha gave a grim smile, turning her gaze back to the window. "But he is very capable. I do hope he manages to find a wife to bring many children into such a large home. How lonely his life would be without a family."

Jane shifted uncomfortably in her seat, and Lady Tabitha chuckled. "Yes, I know. Lord Barnet."

Jane nodded, allowing herself to admire the exterior of the estate as the carriage came up the drive. Though it was beautiful, there was a certain haunting quality to it, a fascinating dreariness that emanated from the stone facade. As Jane gazed upon the house, Lord Seaford stepped out the front doors to approach their carriage. Watching him descend the steps, Jane decided that the cheerful, friendly owner did not suit the dark house at all.

Lord Seaford wore a black top hat, hiding his dark curls. He smiled as he stepped up to the door of the carriage, his gaze lingering on Jane. She looked down, unsettled by the admiration in his eyes. He extended his hand to help her down from the carriage. She had half a mind to ignore it but thought better of it. Lady Tabitha would never forgive her if she did.

Do not encourage him, she reminded herself as she took his hand, avoiding his eyes. The moment her feet touched the ground she let go of him.

"Miss Milton," he said, calling her gaze to his. "I cannot wait for you to meet my horses. I brought my own from my home in Brighton, but the horses of Pengrave are beautiful creatures as well."

She gave him a doubtful look. "They cannot possibly be better than my horses in Ashford."

He laughed, a loud and hearty sound. She had not expected him to laugh.

Something about the sound encouraged her to continue. "I am not jesting. My horses are better than yours. I am certain."

He tipped his head to the side, studying her as if she were a mysterious insect. Amusement gleamed in his eyes. "I can't believe such a claim."

"You ought to believe it."

"And betray my dear horses?" Lord Seaford pressed his hand to his heart, shaking his head in mock regret. "I could never let them hear me surrender their superiority to yours."

A smile tugged on Jane's lips. "If you are suggesting that your horses understand the English language, then perhaps they are indeed superior to mine."

He threw his head back, releasing another loud laugh. Against her will, her face broke into a smile as she watched him laughing. She had never heard such a contagious laugh. She quickly hid her smile when he looked at her again.

Did he truly find her so humorous? It was strange. She had always remained prim and quiet in the company of gentlemen—usually because she hoped to impress them, and her mother had coached her that men objected to loud laughter and outspoken words. She reminded herself that she had no desire to impress Lord Seaford, so she could speak her mind as she pleased. She quite liked the freedom.

Still chuckling, he helped his grandmother descend from the carriage, casting Jane a look of amusement over his shoulder. "I see we are finally in agreement. My horses are superior."

Jane shook her head. "I only said they would be superior if they understood the English language."

"They do."

She narrowed her eyes at him. "I will require proof of that."

"Proof? Have you no faith in my word?" Lord Seaford feigned offense, a pretend scowl scrunching his brow. Jane had never seen such an expressive face. Laughter bubbled in her chest, but she didn't let it escape.

"I am not yet convinced of your trustworthiness," she said.

"I will vouch for him," Lady Tabitha said, a mischievous grin on her lips as she watched them. "He is the most honorable and honest man you will ever meet."

Jane raised one eyebrow at Lord Seaford, taking note of the laughter twitching on his lips. "I daresay that is not the face of an honest man."

A gust of wind stole Lord Seaford's hat, and it went spinning into the air behind him. Leaves spiraled up from the ground as he chased it, his long limbs flailing. The laughter Jane had been holding threatened to break the surface once again.

He scooped his hat up from the distant ground, smoothing his hair before replacing the hat on his head. Lady Tabitha fell into laughter, and he joined her. Jane bit her lip to keep from grinning.

"Misfortune favors the wicked, Lord Seaford," Jane called. "Your dishonesty has been discovered."

His face, though flushed with embarrassment, still smiled. "You have caught me, Miss Milton."

She grinned in triumph before stopping herself. She could not let him see that she had been entertained by their conversation, strange as it was. He would likely take her smiles as encouragement, and that was the last thing she wanted. Lord Seaford was a strange man. Endearing and humorous at times, but certainly strange. She eyed him carefully as he stepped toward her. "Shall we take our ride?" His gaze shifted to his grandmother and back to Jane.

Jane gave a polite nod, reluctantly taking his arm as he extended it to her.

To reach the stables on the far side of the property, they crossed through the house. Jane could not hide her amazement at the interior of the home. The walls stretched high, ending in domed ceilings. The marble floors were black and white, shining as if they had been freshly polished. Portraits of ancient faces lined the walls as they made their way past the grand staircase and toward the back door. The trio's footsteps echoed in the vast space.

When they stepped outside through the back door, Jane glanced at Lord Seaford. She almost told him how beautiful his home was but held her tongue. Would he interpret such a compliment to mean she wished to live there? To be mistress of Pengrave? She didn't dare take the risk.

Inside the stables, two grooms were busy at work. Light filtered through the upper windows, illuminating the dust and dirt that floated in the air above the numerous horses. Lord Seaford approached the nearest stall, stroking a tan horse between the eyes.

"Brimmer does not take well to strangers." He cast Jane a look of warning. "I would not recommend you choose him for your ride."

He proceeded to introduce Jane and Lady Tabitha to every horse in the stables, calling them each by name. She paused to admire each one, a surge of longing rising within her for her own horse, Locket. It would be months before she could ride him again. She reminded herself that if she met with success here in Brighton, she would be riding Locket with Lord Barnet at her side on his own matching sleek black horse.

When all the horses had been introduced, Jane selected the horse that Lord Seaford had warned her not to choose. Brimmer. He seemed surprised at her choice, hesitation hovering in his gaze. He selected a gentle mare for his grandmother, a wary look on his face as he watched Jane prepare to mount her horse.

"Are you certain you don't wish to ride Newton? He is very well-mannered."

Jane stepped on the mounting block, settling on the saddle of Brimmer. The horse shifted restlessly. "If I wished for well-mannered company I would be in the drawing room with a group of polite young ladies with a tea tray between us." She stroked the horse's head, leaning forward to whisper reassurances in its ear. The horse seemed to relax.

Lord Seaford laughed, a look of shock lifting his expression. "If you manage to train my horses to understand English, by George, I'll believe you are capable of anything!"

She snuck a glance at his face, and a hint of panic struck her as she noticed the admiration there. She was not doing a sufficient job of deferring Lord Seaford's attention. She needed to halt his favor of her before her parents could witness it again. Scrambling for an idea, she decided upon showcasing her fiercest flaw, her most dreaded deterrent. Her hair.

As Lord Seaford mounted his horse beside her, she surveyed the wide property. If she rode fast enough, she could blame the wind for unraveling the secure, neat twist Suzanne had styled her hair in beneath her hat. Surely if Lord Seaford saw the wild disaster that grew from her head he would find her far less appealing.

With a firm grip on the reins, Jane let her horse have his head, first trotting, then soaring across the trimmed grass. The horse was difficult to manage at first, but quickly grew used to her touch. The cold wind whipped at her hat, throwing it from her head like Lord Seaford's had just moments before. With one hand, she discreetly loosened the pins in her hair, shaking her head in the wind.

As expected, her fiery locks slipped out of confinement, splaying out all over her head as the wind tore through them. She laughed to herself as she approached the trees behind the property. Lord Seaford and Lady Tabitha were far behind, and Jane hoped Lord Seaford found her to be a madwoman for racing off in such an improper manner. Her hair certainly looked like it could belong to a madwoman. She only hoped Lady Tabitha would not send her back to Ashford for her terrible behavior.

She circled around to face her companions, eager to see the horror on Lord Seaford's face. She was shocked to see his smile of pure delight as he approached. He slowed his horse, coming to a halt in front of her. She instinctively touched her hair, suddenly self-conscious of it—the abundance of it—hanging wildly around her shoulders. Lady Tabitha still remained near the stables, moving at a sedate pace.

"You continue to surprise me, Miss Milton," Lord Seaford said, his voice mingled with a laugh. His horse paced in a circle as he watched her, sweeping his gaze over her hair. She waited for the look of dismay to come, but it never did. Lord Seaford continued to stare at her with unyielding fascination, not bothering to hide it. Jane wondered if he was capable of hiding a single emotion he felt. He did not seem inclined to.

Jane, however, had learned to do so at a young age, faced with countless critiques from her parents and sisters.

"You have managed to tame Brimmer. Did I mention that he is among my favorites of my horses?"

Jane rubbed her hand over Brimmer's head, smiling gingerly at the horse. "He is beautiful."

When she glanced up, she found Lord Seaford's gaze. "Indeed," he said, his eyes lingering on her face.

Despite her every effort to stop it, Jane felt her cheeks warm. She could only hope they were not as pink as Lord Seaford's. She cursed herself for allowing him to affect her, and for allowing his subtle compliment to give her any sense of flattery. This was Lord Seaford! If the words had come from Lord Barnet she might have understood her reaction. But not from the ridiculous, awkward, yet strangely endearing marquess. She tore her eyes away from him, forcing her cheeks to cool.

He tightened his reins, a soft smile lifting his lips as he stared at her. "I never thought it possible to grow attached to someone in such a brief period of time."

Her heart leapt in panic. "What?"

"Brimmer," he said in a quick voice, motioning at her horse. "And the other horses of Pengrave. They have been my closest confidants and friends in the time I have spent adjusting to this new life."

"Confidants?"

He grinned. "Yes. As I said before, they understand my words, yet they cannot speak them in return. There has never been a greater friend to keep a secret than a Pengrave horse."

Jane rolled her eyes—she could not help herself.

Lord Seaford gave a look of mock surprise. "You still doubt my words?"

"I require proof," she reminded him.

He straightened his posture on his saddle. "Very well. I will prove to you that my horses are of the highest intellect in all of England."

Jane watched with amusement as he leaned forward, putting his mouth near the ear of his horse. His hands pulled back on the reins, keeping his horse still. He threw Jane a pompous smirk as he reached into his jacket and withdrew two small apples.

He placed one apple in his fist, holding it in front of the muzzle of his horse. In a whisper, but loud enough for Jane to hear, he said, "If you understand what I am speaking to you, eat this apple."

He uncurled his fingers and the horse tentatively opened its mouth, swiping the apple from Lord Seaford's palm. He raised one eyebrow at Jane, his eyes glinting with a challenge.

Jane pressed her lips together in an effort to contain her laugh, but it was futile. She gave a loud giggle, quickly covering her mouth.

Lord Seaford surrendered his charade, bursting into laughter. His laugh sent Jane into another bout of giggles. She picked up the reins, steering her horse away from Lord Seaford so he wouldn't see her.

"Miss Milton!" he said through a laugh, "where are you going?"

Jane shook her head hard, her hair whipping around her shoulders as she laughed. She pressed a hand to her stomach, the ache from her laughter making it difficult to breathe. It was Lord Seaford's expression more than anything else that had sent her plummeting into such a state. She took a deep breath, attempting to correct her expression before circling her horse to face him again.

With a grin, he extended the second apple to his horse. "Miss Milton has a lovely laugh, do you agree?" The horse eagerly stole the apple from Lord Seaford's hand, juice spraying out the sides of its mouth.

Lord Seaford threw his hands in the air, turning his smile to Jane. "You have your proof."

She pressed down her giggles. What had happened? She had strayed far from her plan of how she would act around him. She had planned to remain aloof and cold, but he had somehow managed to undo all her preparation. Dread poured through her. It needed to stop.

"The only thing you have proven is that your horses like apples, my lord," she said.

A teasing glint entered his eyes. "What if I were to tell you that *this* horse regularly refuses apples?"

"Then I would deem you dishonest, contrary to your grandmother's opinion."

Lord Seaford chuckled, glancing over his shoulder at the place where his grandmother sat atop her horse. She did not seem to have moved since Jane had last seen her. Was she intentionally leaving Jane alone with Lord Seaford? Vexation welled up inside her. Why did everyone endorse the match?

"I must take my leave," she said. "I do not feel well."

His smile dropped. "Do you need water? Or food? I will send a servant immediately."

"No, thank you. I simply need to return to Brighton."

Lord Seaford nodded, his inability to hide his emotions displayed yet again in his disappointed frown. Jane ignored the pang of regret that stabbed her as they turned their horses back toward the stables. If her parents asked why she had returned to Brighton after such a short time, she would say that Lord Seaford had no longer appeared interested in her.

Perhaps by the ball that night her parents would support her pursuit of Lord Barnet once again and forget Lord Seaford even existed.

They reached the stables and he helped her dismount, gripping her waist as he lowered her to the ground. Reluctant at first, Lady Tabitha finally agreed to return to Brighton. Jane's illness was not a complete lie. Her stomach flipped and twisted at the thought of facing Lord Barnet that night. It was her first chance. Perhaps her only chance, and she could not ruin it.

Nothing could ruin it.

Lord Seaford helped Jane into the carriage, bidding her farewell with a smile. She gave him a brief smile in return, her gaze hovering on his eyes, and the depth that sparked in them.

She turned to the opposite window, unwilling to find

anything else about Lord Seaford to admire. But her resolve did not last long. A light grin tugged at her lips as the carriage pulled away from Pengrave. She had never met a man that behaved like Lord Seaford, much less a man of title. He laughed at odd moments, smiled at nearly *every* moment, and said the most peculiar and entertaining things.

He claimed that she had often surprised him, but she found that he was surprising her. She hated to admit it to herself, but she was a touch flattered that he held her in high regard. She had little experience being admired. That was the thing about Lord Seaford that surprised her most of all.

As she watched Pengrave grow smaller in the distance, she wondered in what other ways he might surprise her. She stopped herself, pushing Lord Seaford from her mind. She needed to focus on more important matters: the ball at Clemsworth, impressing a viscount, and taming her now catastrophic hair. Hope bloomed inside her. Her fortune was bound to change tonight—she could feel it in the wind.

Chapter 9

Philip groaned, leaning toward his reflection in the mirror in his bedchamber. He had made a complete bufflehead of himself with Miss Milton. He was certain her 'illness' had only been an excuse to escape his presence.

First he had lost his hat, then he had concocted the ridiculous story that his horses could understand English, and his attempted compliments toward Miss Milton had not been well received. He rubbed the side of his face.

"You are a bufflehead," he said in a loud voice, staring into the wide eyes of his reflection. His jaw tightened. But how could he give up on her? He was entirely and irrevocably smitten with Miss Jane Milton. He had never seen a woman ride so fearlessly. She had certainly surprised him with her skill riding Brimmer, and he had concluded that she was just as free-spirited as the horse.

And she was beautiful. Her smile and laugh had nearly undone him.

He sat down at his desk, placing his face in his hands. Regret poured through him as he thought of all the things he should have done and said differently. Would he have another opportunity? Considering her swift departure that morning he doubted she wanted to see him again. He should have offered her more words of flattery, as Lord Ramsbury had advised him. If only he possessed a fraction of that man's talent. He could win Miss Milton's heart for certain.

Pacing the room, he glanced at his pocket watch. It read noon. He had eight hours to prepare for the ball at Clemsworth—eight hours to plan his next move. Earning the favor of Miss Milton was like an elaborate game of chess, strategic and meticulous, with many worthy and skilled opponents. Fear was his greatest opponent.

His game of chess with Lord Ramsbury flashed in his mind, his instructor's words playing across his mind like a melody: *If you kiss her properly, away from the watchful eye of society, you will have become a real marquess, and a real man... and you will have communicated to Miss Milton in the most concise way of your affection.*

Philip swallowed, his throat suddenly dry. Could Lord Ramsbury have been right? No matter what Philip did, he could not seem to convey to her his feelings. He paused at the window, looking down at the front property and the groundskeeper who stood below watering the bushes. The silence of the house was deafening, planting seeds of doubt in his mind. Miss Milton could never care for him. To steal a kiss from a woman that did not desire him would be wicked and rakish. Philip was not that man.

To accept defeat with grace was a skill his mother had

taught him at a young age. He could still remember the intensity of her brown eyes as she held him by the shoulders. He had been learning croquet with his cousins that had come to Brighton. He had lost the game by one point and was as devastated as a ten-year-old boy could be over a trivial thing, sitting in the dirt and holding back tears. "You will be much happier if you accept your loss with grace," his mother had said. "Now dust off your breeches and play again."

His mother's loss had come four years later, and he had tried to have grace. But then his father had followed, and Philip fell apart. There had been little else left that he cared for, and he had considered himself defeated by life. It had taken all he had. When he moved to live with his grandmother, she had not tolerated his depressed state, echoing his mother's words with her actions. *Now dust off your breeches and play again.*

Tonight at the ball he would give his last attempt at wooing Miss Milton. If she still remained aloof, he would accept his defeat with grace. More likely than not, Miss Milton's feelings would not change, no matter what he did. Even if he took Lord Ramsbury's advice, he knew a simple kiss could not bring about so much change. Could it?

His pacing took him back to the mirror, where he shook his head at his reflection. "No," he said, raising a scolding finger at himself, his eyes wide. "You are not a scoundrel. A bufflehead, yes, but not a scoundrel."

Philip escaped his room with large strides before he could convince himself otherwise. In the eight hours that followed he would remain occupied with managing his estate. There was much to learn, and he needed a distraction from Miss Milton and her enchanting hair and piercing eyes. His heart flipped. Her pending rejection loomed over him, but he ignored it. At least he could sympathize with Ramsbury, who had been rejected by Miss Amelia Buxton.

Philip was not alone.

With a deep breath, he made his way to Pengrave's library.

Chapter 10

Sitting within Lady Tabitha's carriage, Jane tugged on her gloves with vigor, staring at the light within the windows of Clemsworth. Her heart thudded, banging against her ribs like a drum. The dark sky intensified the candlelight, and the house loomed like a monster with dozens of glowing windows for eyes, waiting to devour Jane and every drop of hope that remained within her.

Lord Barnet was within those walls, she was sure of it. She imagined him standing within a crowd, drawing the eyes of every woman in attendance with his dark and mysterious air, the green of his eyes stealing every heart that dared to look within them.

"You look lovely, Miss Milton," Lady Tabitha said from the seat across from her. Jane could barely distinguish her outline in the dark. "If Lord Barnet does not see that, then surely another man will."

"Thank you. That is very kind." Jane did not care if another man did. She had not come to Brighton for *another* man. Her future balanced on this one evening, this one ball, and one opportunity. Anxiety threatened to overwhelm her.

Her mother had been disappointed in her early arrival from her ride with Lord Seaford that morning but had not shown the surrender Jane had hoped for. If anything, her mother had become more determined to make Jane impress Lord Seaford.

Per her mother's instruction, Jane wore a satin white gown with golden embroidery and a gold sash at the waist. A fanciful lace adorned her neck, and her hair had been tamed to perfection by Susanne. She had never felt more beautiful. Within the walls of Lady Tabitha's home, she had been saturated with confidence, but here, approaching Clemsworth in the dark, she felt that confidence shriveling.

As they descended from the carriage, Jane wrapped her red shawl loosely around her shoulders, combatting the chilled autumn air. Lady Tabitha clung to Jane's arm, smiling at the people they passed on their way to the entrance.

Jane struggled to calm her racing heart and to maintain her footing on the path as her legs shook. Would Lord Barnet even remember her? She hushed her fears, reminding herself that it had only been a fortnight since he had dined with her family.

She lifted her skirts as she and Lady Tabitha climbed the steps to the door. The butler ushered the new group as they arrived, sending them down the west hall to the ballroom. Jane listened to the lively music and laughter as it wafted through the air of the grand home. Clemsworth was not as large as Pengrave but was equal in charm. It was no wonder Lord Ramsbury put on such pompous airs. As Jane considered Lord Seaford, his level of humility struck her with curiosity. He had seemed wary to even claim the land and property of Pengrave as his own.

She quickly stopped herself. She was not supposed to be thinking of Lord Seaford at this moment.

The doors of the ballroom opened into a wide and crowded space, filled with hundreds of guests. Jane squared her shoulders, willing herself to be more confident than she felt. Candlelight flooded the room from the intricate sconces on the wall, reflecting off the golden drapes that framed the windows. Her eyes searched the room for any sign of Lord Barnet, but there were many gentlemen in attendance, many of which were just as tall as Lord Barnet. Those that were not dancing the quadrille stood on the outskirts of the room, watching the dancers with pleasant smiles.

The women that danced moved with grace, their steps light and flawless, their perfect and neutral curls bouncing, their cheeks flushed with exertion. The men smiled at their partners, but Jane did not see Lord Barnet's smile among them.

Lady Tabitha leaned toward Jane. "Is he here?" she whispered.

Jane rose on her toes, eyeing a dark-haired gentleman that passed in front of her. It was not Lord Barnet. "I have not seen him."

Lady Tabitha tugged on Jane's elbow, pulling her to an empty space beside the north wall. "We need a clearer vantage point, that is all." As if she knew who she was searching for, Lady Tabitha squinted at the crowd. "Is that him?" she asked, far too loudly, pointing at a man that stood against the opposite wall.

"No."

Jane's gaze caught on a set of broad shoulders, turned away from her. Her heart leapt. The dark hair and height were familiar. The man beside him spoke, and he turned to listen, giving Jane a glance at his profile.

It was him. Lord Barnet was here.

Jane wanted to turn and run out of the ballroom. Her legs began shaking again, and she rotated to face Lady Tabitha.

She must have noticed the paleness of Jane's face, or the fear in her eyes, for she gave a deep chuckle. "I suspect you have found him."

There was still time for Jane to escape. Lord Barnet had not seen her yet. What had she been thinking coming all the way to Brighton for him? She had planned her life around a man that stood miles above her in status and beauty—a man that would never blink in her direction. She calmed her nerves, reminding herself that he had seemed somewhat interested in her that night he had come to dinner.

"He is even more handsome than you described him," Lady Tabitha said, delight in her voice. Jane watched Lord Barnet as he gave a polite smile to the man beside him. He spoke, but Jane was too far away to hear. She gazed at him, unable to think or breathe.

"I should like you to introduce him to me." Lady Tabitha took a step toward him.

Jane reached out in panic, grabbing her by the sleeve. "No!"

Lady Tabitha's eyes widened. Jane released her, smoothing out the lace of her puce sleeve. "I mean… I must plan my words carefully first."

"I suspect you have been planning your words since you departed from Ashford, Miss Milton. There is nothing more to plan. Come now." Lady Tabitha walked in the direction of Lord Barnet, purpose in her small, shuffling strides. Jane froze, torn between remaining where she was or chasing after Lady Tabitha.

Jane took a deep breath of fortitude. She could not waste another moment being a coward. She squeezed her way past a group of young ladies, most of which had set their eyes upon Lord Barnet, whispering to one another behind gloved hands.

Jane skirted in front of Lady Tabitha, only five feet away from Lord Barnet. His back still faced her, so she stepped past the group of ladies on his other side. He faced her fully now, and she dared to look up at his face. He had not seen her yet.

The women that had been watching him cast her a look of dismay, and a bit of jealousy, as she took a step closer to him. She supposed they had been waiting all night to make his acquaintance so they could speak with him, but Jane had the advantage of already being introduced. She had grown up beside him and grown up admiring him. It was only fair that she should get to speak with him first.

She could hear nothing but her pulse as it pounded past her ears. Lady Tabitha stood to the left of Jane, waiting in silence for Lord Barnet to notice them. Would he see her? Would he even acknowledge her?

Just as the question crossed her mind, his eyes found Jane's. Recognition flashed in his gaze, wrought with heavy confusion.

She gave a shaky smile, nodding at him in greeting.

"Lord Barnet," she squeaked, stepping up beside him. She looked up—far up—at his face. "I thought we might stumble upon one another here in Brighton."

He smoothed his expression, just a slight frown marking his brow. "Miss Milton. I must confess I am surprised to see you away from Ashford. What brought you to Brighton?"

She stared at the streaks of green and blue in his eyes, framed by dark and thick lashes. Her head swam with a string of incoherent replies she might give him, settling on the one she had practiced. "I am serving as a companion to Lady Tabitha." She gestured at the woman beside her. "She is the grandmother of my dear friend Caroline Easton of Ashford. Miss Easton is the one who informed me of her grandmother's need." Jane cleared her throat, hoping that doing so would stop the shaking in her voice.

"I see." Lord Barnet nodded at Lady Tabitha, who bobbed her head at him in return.

"It is wonderful to make your acquaintance, Lord Barnet," Lady Tabitha said. Jane caught the glance Lady Tabitha threw her, a gleam of approval in her eyes.

"A pleasure," he said. Rubbing his jaw in thought, he turned his attention back to Jane. "Why did you not speak of your intention to travel to Brighton when I dined with your family? I would have been glad to hear of it."

Hope surged in her chest as she examined his face. "Truly?"

"Indeed. It is refreshing to see a familiar face among so many strangers." Lord Barnet gave a small smile, and Jane felt her knees wobble.

"I felt the same when I saw you, my lord." She tried to return his smile, but her face felt as if it had been dipped in fire, crisp and tight and warm with a raging blush.

She searched for something else to say. "My mother and father accompanied me here but will be departing at first light tomorrow."

Lord Barnet surveyed the crowd. The moment his gaze left Jane's face she released the breath she had been holding, willing her cheeks to cool. "Ah, are they here at Clemsworth?" he asked. "I am fond of Mr. and Mrs. Milton. They have always treated me well."

Jane's parents had not expressed their intent to go to the ball, though the invitation had been extended to them. They had been at the shops in town all day, and they usually liked to retire early. Jane was relieved to hear that they were unlikely to be in attendance.

"My parents are currently at Lady Tabitha's residence, I believe. They have been very occupied these last two days and desired a long rest before their travel home tomorrow." Jane was proud of how calm her voice sounded.

Lord Barnet gave her another smile, making her stomach flutter violently. Would he ask her for a dance? She stared up at him, hoping, waiting.

"It is my sincere hope that your parents return to Ashford in safety. Please wish them well for me," he said.

Jane nodded. "Of course. They will be glad to hear from you."

Lord Barnet gave her a quick bow, ending their conversation. He turned back to the man with whom he had been conversing before.

Jane's face fell. Was that all? Every word she had hoped and imagined him to speak to her had just been trampled in her mind. She had imagined that he would compliment her, gaze into her eyes, cast her a charming smile, and ask her for at least one dance. She closed her eyes, fighting back the tears that burned there. She reminded herself that this had been their first meeting in Brighton. There would be more opportunities.

"Pin the skirts of your dress about your feet," Lady Tabitha whispered as they walked away from Lord Barnet. "You must do so if you wish to signify your intention to dance."

Jane looked at the guests in the room, spotting several young ladies engaged in the current dance with their skirts pinned so they did not drag on the floor. Lady Tabitha held up a fistful of pins, ushering Jane to the wall. Working quickly, Lady Tabitha pinned Jane's skirts in four places, freeing her feet from the layers of white and gold fabric.

"You must always come prepared." Lady Tabitha straightened with a grunt. Placing her hands on her hips, she examined her work. Jane conjured up a smile, kicking her foot out from beneath her gown.

Jane sighed. "Thank you, but I'm afraid hope is lost. Lord Barnet does not find me attractive at all."

Lady Tabitha tapped her chin. "I would not eliminate the possibility just yet."

"Do you think there is hope?"

"He could simply be shy."

Jane felt a touch on her shoulder, so gentle she could have mistaken it for the brush of her sleeve. As she turned, she was surprised to find the clear brown eyes of Lord Seaford, looking down into hers. His mouth spread into a crooked smile, a dimple denting his right cheek.

"Miss Milton." Even as he said her name his face brightened. "You look very lovely this evening. Although I must say I preferred your hair in the style you had this morning while riding." His eyes glinted teasingly.

She lacked the energy to react. Her eyes slid to Lord

Barnet, and his gaze met hers across the room. She watched as he looked at Lord Seaford, his eyes lingering on him with surprise.

"But I do not mean to say that this style is not also becoming," Lord Seaford stammered, gesturing at her head. "I only mean to say that your hair will look beautiful no matter how it is arranged."

Jane hardly heard him. Lord Barnet still conversed with his friend, but his eyes continually shifted to Lord Seaford. Did Jane see a hint of jealousy? It couldn't be possible. Her heart thudded. She straightened her posture, new confidence surging within her chest.

"That is very kind of you to say, Lord Seaford." She gave him a bright smile. "But my hair could not have looked more becoming atop that horse than you looked while chasing after your hat."

He threw his head back in laughter, and Jane took a moment to glance at Lord Barnet. He still watched them, his jaw tightening at his eyes focused on Lord Seaford. Perhaps his regard for her had not just been in her imagination. He didn't express his interest in the way that Lord Seaford did. Jane had watched Lord Barnet in his interactions with her sisters, and he had always seemed bored and detached. But with Jane, he had been attentive, offering small smiles and kind words. He was not obvious in his attention, but it was there, hiding behind his mysterious, brooding facade. Perhaps if he saw her interacting with Lord Seaford, it would instill a bit of urgency within him. If she could manage to fuel his jealousy, he might request a dance of her yet.

Lord Seaford pressed his lips together, suppressing his smile. "I am in earnest, Miss Milton. You are beautiful."

Jane's eyes flew back up to his. His face reddened slightly, but he maintained her gaze. "I would like to request the honor of a dance," he said.

"The honor would be mine." Jane tried to appear excited. She hoped Lord Barnet had overheard Lord Seaford. "I should like to dance the cotillion with you."

His eyes glinted with a mixture of surprise and relief. "I would like that very much. If you are as skilled a dancer as you are a singer and rider, I will declare you to be the most accomplished lady of my acquaintance."

Jane smiled up at him, no longer forcing herself to resist the infectious quality of his grin. Lord Barnet still watched them, and it pushed her forward. "You have too many kind words for me tonight, my lord."

He shrugged, leaning his head down. "If you wish for me to stop you might consider being less remarkable."

The sincerity in his expression brought a blush to Jane's cheeks. It would contribute nicely to her act. Was it an act? The leap of her heart felt very real as Lord Seaford's eyes gazed into hers.

Jane looked away fast, catching the eye of Lady Tabitha, momentarily taken aback by the look of disapproval on her face. Jane had forgotten the woman still stood beside them. She lifted one pale eyebrow. Did she realize Jane's designs?

"Your grandmother could attest that I am not all that remarkable," Jane said.

Lady Tabitha cleared her expression when her grandson turned his gaze to her. "Oh, yes. Miss Milton is much less remarkable than you think."

Jane felt the honesty behind the words, guilt stabbing her through the heart. She gave a hard laugh, vastly uncomfortable under Lady Tabitha's glare.

"It is my turn to doubt your words, grandmother," he said with a chuckle.

Jane chewed her lip. Was it so cruel to give Lord Seaford the impression that she welcomed his attention if it was only for one evening? She would only continue with her act until Lord Barnet realized that he had a competitor. Lord Seaford couldn't expect to win against Lord Barnet, could he? He would accept his defeat without a second thought.

Jane's efforts to justify her wickedness only brought about more guilt. She shifted on her feet, flicking her gaze to Lord Barnet. He had started moving closer, working his way through the crowd, pausing to greet his acquaintances. His eyes found hers.

She turned her smile on Lord Seaford, ignoring Lady Tabitha's subtle efforts to unnerve her. "I don't have a reason to believe a single word you say after you tried to convince me your horses possessed human intellect. Why should I believe you when you offer this flattery of me?"

Jane didn't have experience flirting with gentlemen, but each of her sisters had mastered the talent, and Jane had witnessed their skill on many occasions. She tried to imitate the demure glances and teasing words she had seen them utilize.

Lord Seaford considered her words, his brow furrowing. He was silent for a long moment before he spoke again. "I wish I could prove my words to you." He stopped, scowling at the ground. "Will you excuse me, Miss Milton?"

Her smile faltered. "Very well."

"I will return for our dance." He threw her a lingering glance before turning around and pushing through the crowd to his unknown destination. She puzzled over his abrupt departure, watching his back until she lost him in the crowd. As she turned to find Lord Barnet, her heart skipped. He stood less than ten feet away.

Her hope quickly fell when she realized that he was speaking to a group of young ladies, all of which were wholly captivated by him. Jane puffed out a breath of frustration, searching the room for Lord Seaford. Without him she could not make Lord Barnet envious enough to approach her.

She hoped he would return soon. The attention of a marquess could only make her more desirable.

Jane dared a look at Lady Tabitha. "At least your grandson has taken note of my pinned skirts and asked me to dance."

Lady Tabitha clamped her lips shut, as if she didn't wish to speak the words that hid behind them. She seemed to change her mind, raising a scolding finger at Jane. "My Philip is a good man. You are fortunate to have his favor. Do not abuse it."

Jane's cheeks flamed. So Lady Tabitha had discerned her true motive in flirting with Lord Seaford.

"Misfortune favors the wicked," Lady Tabitha said, echoing Jane's words from that morning.

Jane remained silent. Yes, her manipulation of Lord Seaford was certainly wicked, but how could it bring about misfortune? Lord Barnet had noticed her, and she had seen the jealousy in his eyes. It was only a matter of time before he swept himself between her and Lord Seaford. Her act would only carry on for a short time.

Accepting her justification, she eagerly awaited Lord Seaford's return.

Chapter 11

Wiping the perspiration from his brow, Philip paced the ballroom, searching for Lord Ramsbury. He could find him nowhere. *Blast it.* This was Lord Ramsbury's ball! How could he not be in attendance?

Philip exited through the main doors, walking down the vast hallway in search of his friend. Miss Milton had changed drastically since that morning. He had come to the ball prepared for defeat, but now… defeat was not so certain. What had changed? He could scarcely believe it when she had first smiled at him that night. She had never offered a smile so readily. Had his efforts that morning been effective? Perhaps she truly had been feeling ill. Her warm reception of him at the ball had given him the fortitude to offer the compliments he had been holding back.

But were his words enough?

Since the moment he had seen her walk in the ballroom, he had been unable to thwart his consideration of Lord Rambsury's advice. Already Philip had seen Miss Milton conversing with the Viscount of Barnet. His time was short if he wished to win her heart before anyone else.

Philip circled the empty hall again, pausing at the open door of the dining room. Lord Ramsbury sat at the table alone with a tall glass of port. Two empty glasses lay on their sides in front of him.

"Edward?" Philip scowled, stepping into the room. Lord Ramsbury looked up, his eyes lazy and dull.

"What the devil are you doing?" Philip asked. "Why are you not at the ball?"

Lord Ramsbury slouched in his chair, sipping from his glass. "I do not see the motivation to socialize tonight, Seaford."

"And why is that?"

Lord Ramsbury sat forward, digging his index finger into the wood of the table, his balance wavering in his chair. "Every woman I meet is the same. She wants my title. She wants this estate. She desires the prestige of a match with me," he said, his words slurred. "She thrives off of my flattery rather than… resisting it. Miss Buxton hated when I flattered her," he gave a hard laugh. "And for a moment I thought she believed me to be something more than the eldest son of an earl." He glanced up at Philip. "I cannot expect that there is a woman in that ballroom that will compare to her."

Philip had never seen Lord Ramsbury so uncollected. He took a large swig from his glass.

"Shouldn't you be charming Miss Milton?" he said.

Philip rubbed his forehead, the words of encouragement he had been about to offer Lord Ramsbury fleeing his mind. "I should, but I do not know how."

"Have you come to tell me I was correct?"

"No, I—"

"Kiss the woman, Seaford." Lord Ramsbury said in a tired voice. "Now. Before I do it myself."

Philip crossed his arms. "You wouldn't."

Lord Ramsbury smiled, tracing the rim of his glass with one finger.

Philip was beginning to suspect he would.

"I only mean to give you a bit of urgency. There could be another man within that ballroom as we speak, searching for an opportunity to speak with her, to dance with her, to invite her to come riding *without* his grandmother. If you are going to win her heart, now is the moment. You must employ every tactic."

Philip glanced at the door, his jaw tightening. Could he really find the courage? He had never been one to break the rules of society, but here he was, considering the unthinkable.

A simple kiss.

But it was not just a simple kiss. He would have to lead her away, unchaperoned. If they were seen her reputation would be in tatters. How could he take the risk? He wouldn't. With firm resolve, he nodded in farewell to Lord Ramsbury.

"I must return to the ballroom for my dance with Miss Milton."

Lord Ramsbury shook his head in disapproval. "A dance will not be enough."

Philip ignored him, retracing his steps down the deserted hallway, following the music that flowed from the ballroom. At the doors, he took a deep breath. He was still not accustomed to the attention he received when he entered a room. Whether it was a drawing room, assembly room, card room, or ballroom, he attracted the same gazes of admiration from strangers. They did not know him. Why should they admire him now after he had grown up in this town, receiving no such attention? Why should they admire him now simply because he bore a title? It sickened him. He sympathized with Lord Ramsbury more than ever. Would he ever be anything but a marquess in the eyes of society?

As he stepped back into the ballroom, he caught the gazes of several young ladies as he searched for Miss Milton. He found her, standing against the opposite wall.

When he reached her, she gave him a wide smile. His heart squeezed. He still hadn't grown accustomed to seeing her smile, and it never failed to tug at his composure.

"Did I miss our dance?" he asked.

She shook her head, her ginger curls bouncing. "You have arrived just in time." Her eyes flicked to the left where a group of young ladies stood, surrounding the Viscount of Barnet. She returned her gaze to Philip. "The cotillion is my favorite dance. It is the only dance that I have secured a partner for. All my other dances are unclaimed," she said in a loud voice, her eyes drifting to the left once again.

"Are they?" Philip asked. "May I claim another?"

Her smile pinched. "Oh… yes—of course. But you might dance the cotillion with me before you make such a request. I could very well be a horrendous dancer."

He laughed. "I will take the risk."

Miss Milton pressed her lips together in such an endearing look that he had half a mind to kiss her, right there in the ballroom. He gazed down at her as his laughter subsided, amazed at the openness of her expression. If only he could have more time with her; he might be able to come to know her true character.

Philip followed her eyes as they shifted toward Lord Barnet once again. His heart sank. Lord Barnet had already made a positive impression on Miss Milton. The viscount had only been visiting in Brighton for two weeks, and Philip had made his acquaintance through Lord Ramsbury. The man was silent and serious, always frowning, even now as he watched Miss Milton's interaction with Philip.

Her eyes traveled back to Philip, and she smiled. "Are you certain you wish to take the risk? Your feet may suffer for it."

"My feet?"

"I will likely stomp on them as I struggle through the dance."

Philip laughed, and Miss Milton joined him. His worry subsided. If she were truly so interested in Lord Barnet she would be at his side, not conversing and laughing with Philip.

"Perhaps I have overestimated your talents," he said. "But I will gladly break a toe or two if it means I have the privilege of dancing with you."

Her eyes sparked with genuine amusement, and she examined his feet. "I daresay your boots are thick enough to withstand me."

He laughed at the idea, staring down at her. She was so small; the notion that her weight would break his toes was ridiculous. She lifted her head, tipping her smile up to him. The many shades of red and orange in her hair intensified under the flickering candlelight. Her eyes, wide and blue, trapped him. His heart wavered, and he had to stop his hand from reaching down to brush a loose strand of hair from her forehead.

His boots withstanding Miss Milton was not the issue at all. Philip's heart was in much greater danger than his toes.

For a moment he could think of nothing else. Not the pressure of his title, or the ridiculing eyes of society, or the loneliness of his life. He could only see, hear, feel, and desire the woman in front of him. Just being near her made his heart race and soar with the hope of a happy future. He began to wonder if the accusations of his friends in his adolescence, that he was a romantic, were actually true. He still had no idea if Miss Milton could ever return his feelings.

It would crush him if she rejected him now.

Forgetting himself, his hand lifted to her face, brushing aside that loose strand of hair. Her eyes dropped, her lashes casting down, creating a shadow on her cheeks. He watched as her gaze shifted to the side, her cheeks darkening. Philip followed her gaze to where Lord Barnet had turned around, walking in the direction of the door.

Her posture stiffened, and she took a miniscule step backward. "Lord Seaford, are you familiar with the interior of Clemsworth?"

His hand dropped from her face. He had made her uncomfortable. By touching her so readily he had caused a stir in the ballroom, many sets of eyes resting upon him and Miss Milton. He scolded himself for risking her reputation in such a public way. Society would suspect a settlement between them if he continued displaying his affection, no matter how subtle.

"Yes, I am well acquainted with Lord Ramsbury and have visited many times." He made his voice light, hoping to dispel the awkwardness between them.

"I wondered if you might show me some of the grand rooms," she said, her mouth returning to a smile. "Perhaps the library and music rooms?" Her gaze flickered to the doors that Lord Barnet had just exited through.

"Yes, of course." He threw her a quizzical look. To leave the ballroom alone with him would only cause more of a stir. "I will fetch my grandmother to accompany us."

"No," she stopped him. "I—I would prefer to see the home with you. You alone." She looked up at him from under her lashes, an innocent smile on her lips.

"Are you certain?"

She laughed at the shock of his expression. "Yes! Come along." She started in the direction of the doors, her steps quick and deliberate. Philip followed at a distance, trying to remain inconspicuous to the watchful faces of the room. Men of title often spent parties alone with young ladies, did they not? Lord Ramsbury had said as much. They would return soon, and their excursion would be entirely innocent. There was nothing to worry about.

"Miss Milton," Philip half-whispered as he entered the hall behind her. He stopped himself. Why did he feel the need to whisper? "Where are you going?"

She seemed to be searching for something, rounding a corner and peering carefully around the wall.

"I will direct you to the music room if that is what you are in search of." He chuckled, his boots clicking loudly as he approached her.

She glanced over her shoulder. "Oh, yes. That would be much more productive."

Motioning for her to follow, he set off down the opposite hall. When they passed the dining room, Philip glanced through the open doorway. Lord Ramsbury lay with his head in the bend of his elbow, appearing to be in a deep sleep. Philip's stomach flipped when he recalled the words again. *Kiss her.*

"I should have shown you the music room in Pengrave when you visited this morning," he said in a quick voice, hoping to drown out his thoughts.

"Does it exceed the music room of Clemsworth?" she asked, her eyes still darting in every direction.

"I believe so, but I may be partial to it because it's mine." He laughed.

Miss Milton puffed out a frustrated breath as she glanced around the adjoining hall, but quickly transformed it to a laugh. He wondered what it meant.

"We are nearly there," he said. "It will be well worth the walk, I assure you."

The hall grew dimmer as they walked, and Philip's heart beat louder. Did Miss Milton understand the possible consequences if they were seen unchaperoned? He could already hear the scolding in his grandmother's voice. And the pride in Lord Ramsbury's.

Miss Milton glanced up at him, the smile fading from her features. Did he see disappointment? What had he done wrong? He could almost feel her pulling away from him, resorting to her aloof state once again. He couldn't let it happen. If he lost her now he might never have a chance to explain his feelings again.

"We have arrived," he said in a boisterous voice, hoping to raise her spirits. "May I introduce to you, Miss Milton, the magnificent… the famed… the beautiful music room of Clemsworth." With a wink, he pushed open the heavy wooden door, flooding the dim hallway with various forms of dim light.

The large window on the far wall of the room stood with open drapes, starlight and moonlight filtering through the glass. He froze when he saw several candles resting on the nearby pianoforte, a composition sheet sitting on the music desk. He searched the room with his eyes, relieved to find that they were indeed alone.

He glanced behind him. Miss Milton stood frozen at the door, her eyes wide with fascination. Philip knew that the music room of Pengrave was indeed larger and grander than this one, but he hadn't felt the need to boast of it. The Clemsworth music room housed dozens of instruments, all of which had been freshly cleaned and dusted. The music room of Pengrave had been untouched for years, and Philip's servants were still in the process of recovering it, removing the sheets that had been draped over the instruments for decades. He looked forward to the day his music room would be finished, shining as beautifully as this one as the silver moonlight bounced off the brass and smooth, polished wood.

"It's beautiful," she breathed, stepping farther into the room. She stopped beside him, her mouth hanging open in awe. "I have always wished to learn to play more instruments."

"It is not too late," he said.

She smiled at his encouragement. "Even the violin? I doubt I could learn it without years and years of extensive practice."

"You are capable of more than you realize." Philip turned to face her, tipping his head down to look in her eyes. "I am in earnest. Do not doubt yourself."

She shifted, pulling her gaze away from his. She seemed to realize for the first time that they were alone. "I should leave." Without another word, she turned away from him, her feet clicking swiftly on the marble floor.

Philip's heart sank. Nothing he did could convince her

of his admiration or keep her at his side. *Accept your defeat with grace.* He had spent his entire life accepting his defeat to people with more confidence or wealth or connections. He had given life permission to press him into the heart of despair when he had needed to be strong.

"You cannot leave until I hear your attempt at playing the violin," he said, his voice echoing in the large room.

Her hand froze on the door handle. She raised one eyebrow at him before shaking her head. "It will be the most unpleasant sound you have ever heard."

Gathering his nerve, he took three strides toward her, extending his hand. "I insist."

She looked at the door one last time before letting go of the handle, taking a deep breath. "Very well, but I will make the attempt quick."

"How merciful of you," Philip said with a chuckle.

She gave him another of her suppressed smiles, walking deeper into the room to fetch the nearest violin. She studied the bow, placing the instrument under her chin. Eyeing him with amusement, she placed her fingers on the strings and slid the bow over them, a clear, high-pitched screech cutting the air. She gasped, her smile spreading wide as she made another attempt, the resulting noise resembling a wounded animal.

Philip laughed until his stomach ached as Miss Milton tried one last time, her own laugh ringing through the air. Still chuckling, he took the violin from her hands, giving her a look of mock terror. "You will awaken the dead if you carry on like that."

She gasped before falling into giggles much like the ones she had displayed at Pengrave that morning. "You challenged me to it!"

"I'm afraid I overestimated your ability."

She planted her hands on her hips. "You said I am capable of learning."

"I am not so certain now." Philip gave her a look of pity that he hoped she would see as the jest that it was. He walked closer to her, pushed forward by an unknown force, his steps slow and careful.

She gaped at him. "You said I am capable of more than I realize."

"Did I say that?"

"Yes!"

Philip stood within arms' reach of her now, his smile slipping with her closeness. "You must have imagined it."

"I did not!" She grinned, shaking her head. She jabbed her finger into his chest to emphasize her words, bringing herself even closer to him. He drew a breath as her palm flattened slowly against his chest, her fingers fiddling with his collar. His heart hitched at her touch, picking up speed. She seemed to realize her mistake, her smile faltering as her gaze slid up to his face.

"You are ridiculous," she said in a quiet voice.

"Am I?" Philip tried to laugh, but his breath caught in his throat. His eyes fell to her lips.

"Yes, you are."

"Ridiculous?" He leaned down.

"Have you never heard the word before?"

"Not pertaining to myself."

Philip could see the barriers in her eyes falling, her cold facade melting. He had moved impossibly close, his face now only inches from hers, his mouth hovering near her own. He couldn't think—he could hardly breathe as she released a sigh of frustration, her exhale brushing his neck.

"I do not believe you." Her voice came out quiet, the

last word cracking as he slipped his hand under her chin, tipping her face up to his.

She stared at him, her eyes wide. She licked her lips, stumbling over her words. "Why must you be so vexing?"

Philip's heart thudded as his gaze roamed her features—her wide blue eyes, freckled cheeks, and finally her mouth, opened slightly to offer another rebuke. He was done for. Without his permission, his other hand wrapped slowly around her waist, pulling her against him. Her quick gasp of breath was all he heard before he covered her lips with his.

Her body stiffened in shock before she relaxed, leaning into his arms. Her hands pulled on the fabric of his jacket, returning his kiss with brief fervor. His fingers threaded in her hair. Philip knew he should stop—it was wrong. But the moment the thought crossed his mind, Miss Milton pushed him back with surprising force, sending him stumbling against the pianoforte.

She stared at him in shock, her cheeks blushing a deep red, her hair partially undone, hanging at her shoulders. Guilt burned in her eyes. Philip didn't know what to say. Heavy silence thrummed between them, heightening his sense of regret.

A rustle met his ears from across the room. He turned at the sound, dread pouring through him as a woman stepped out from behind the drapes, her wicked smile coming into light.

Mrs. Milton.

He had been certain the room was empty. His heart raced, and he jerked his gaze to Miss Milton. She had already seen her mother, tears glinting in her eyes.

"Do you have anything to say for yourself, Lord Seaford?" Mrs. Milton asked, her voice wrought with triumph.

He raked his hand through his hair, pacing away from her. He had not intended for their excursion to end in a kiss. "Please," he said. "This was not your daughter's fault."

"Precisely," Mrs. Milton raised her chin. "I expect you to do the honorable thing, Lord Seaford, and my husband will agree. We will not have our daughter's reputation so tarnished."

"You were hiding in the drapes, Mama?" Miss Milton stared at her mother in dismay, tears rolling down her cheeks.

"Only when I heard Lord Seaford's voice outside the room. My suspicion of him has been confirmed. He only meant to lead you away and take advantage of you. Mr. Milton will not stand by such abuse of his daughter, and nor will I. I came to the music room to protect you."

"How did you know we were coming here?" Miss Milton choked. "I didn't know you even came to the ball!"

"Our plans changed. I saw you exit the ballroom with Lord Seaford," her mother said in a proud voice. "I followed, of course, and when you mentioned the music room I found my way here so the two of you would not be unchaperoned. Behind a closed door, no less. I am glad I arrived before Lord Seaford could use you further without offering his hand and fortune." She turned to Philip, her chin raised.

The tears on Miss Milton's cheeks only revealed the truth Philip had been most dreading. She could never love him. She did not even like him. She detested the thought of marrying him. Yet here in the music room, he had kissed her and taken away her choice. How could he have been so thoughtless?

"Well, then, Lord Seaford? Will you marry my Jane to save her from ruin?"

"Mama! I do not wish to marry *him*!" Miss Milton rushed to her mother's side, her words piercing Philip deep in the heart, each word twisting through him like a dull blade. "Can you not speak with Lord Barnet? Perhaps he would save my reputation."

Philip turned away, tightening his jaw against the pain that throbbed in his chest. His face burned with embarrassment and regret.

"No. It must be Lord Seaford. You have been absent together from the party for too long already. You will be missed, and gossip will spread, my dear. When the guests learn that you have been alone together in an empty room, assumptions will be made."

"Lord Barnet left the party as well. I do believe he is interested in me, Mama."

"Enough!"

Philip narrowed his eyes, struggling to see through the tears that clouded his vision. He had ruined Miss Milton's life with a simple kiss. He had subjected her to a life with him that she dreaded, and himself to a life of regret and rejection. Would it be better for Miss Milton to never marry as a result of her ruin, or to spend her life with him? He wasn't certain which fate she looked upon with more dread.

"Lord Seaford." Mrs. Milton recalled his eyes, a sternness lingering there from her conversation with her daughter. "Please put our family's worry to rest. Will you marry Jane?" She extended her hand in her daughter's direction.

He stared at her, willing her eyes to meet his, but she refused, fixing her gaze on the ground as tears fell from her cheeks. Sickened with himself, he covered his face with his hand, struggling to breathe through the torrent of emotions that choked him. He dropped his hand. "I am so sorry, Miss Milton," he said in a hoarse voice. "I never intended for this to happen."

She still refused his gaze.

He squared his shoulders. "I will marry her if it is necessary, but she should not be forced into it."

"You have forced her into it, my lord. Not I."

A fresh wave of grief hit him, straight in the chest. He had never hated himself so much.

"We will plan the ceremony for next week. We must be swift before the town has a moment to gossip. Are you capable of acquiring a special license, my lord?"

Philip watched Miss Milton as she exhaled a quaking breath, wiping the moisture from her face. Her eyes flicked up to his before darting away.

"I will try."

"A small ceremony in the Pengrave drawing room would be sufficient," Mrs. Milton said.

He nodded, lacking the strength to speak. Mrs. Milton, with victory burning in her gaze, took her daughter by the shoulders and guided her out of the room. Philip tried to catch Miss Milton's eyes as she passed, to somehow convey the depth of his regret, of his apology, but she didn't relent. The heavy doors closed behind them, leaving him in utter silence.

He kicked the leg of the pianoforte, dropping to the bench. He leaned his head on his fist, pushing his hair off his forehead. How had it happened so quickly? He had been determined to ignore Lord Ramsbury's advice. Yet still, without thinking, he had stolen a kiss from Miss Milton. He was a cad. A despicable cad.

Philip had gained the information he had sought upon coming to the ball. He now knew for certain Miss Milton's feelings for him. She hated him. Now more than ever. In the moments before their kiss he had suspected her feelings might have been different. And she had even returned his kiss—had she not? But he could never recover from this folly. She would never forgive him.

And, devil take it, he would never heed Lord Ramsbury's advice again.

Chapter 12

Anger pounded against Jane's skull, darkening her vision as her mother pulled her through the halls of Clemsworth. They pushed through the back door of the home. The cold night air did little to cool Jane's cheeks as her mother ushered her into the carriage that awaited them around the front of the estate. Hot tears still spilled over her face, a hoard of emotions cutting through her composure.

Jane didn't know what angered her more, the fact that Lord Seaford had the nerve to kiss her, or the fact that she had—for the briefest moment—welcomed it. She put a hand to her lips in the dark of the carriage, a gentle shiver rolling over her arms. How dare he kiss her? She wiped a new tear that fell down her face, guilt squeezing her heart. She was partially to blame. She had given him the impression that she cared for him, that she welcomed his attention. All to make Lord Barnet jealous. And now she would never be able to court him. She would be married to Lord Seaford by the end of next week.

"I did not know you had the nerve, my dear. Well done." Jane's mother grinned in the dark, just a flash of white teeth and a glint of her eyes.

"The nerve?"

"To ensnare Lord Seaford. To trap him in such an embrace with you, securing an advantageous marriage. I never would have expected you to be so clever."

Jane gritted her teeth. The pleasure her mother took in this arrangement made Jane the angriest of all. Could she not see that Jane was unhappy? Her mother had never cared about a single thing Jane felt, so long as it was beneficial to achieving her own designs.

"I did not intend for this to happen, Mama!"

"Then why did you lead him away to the music room?"

Jane leaned her head back against the cushions, trying to calm her breathing. "I was a fool."

She didn't know what she had been thinking. How could she have been so daft? When she had seen Lord Barnet leaving the ballroom, she had panicked, thinking it wise to follow him. After that, she had stopped trying to encourage Lord Seaford, but he had still made her laugh.

She hadn't meant to. Nor had she meant to kiss him.

She should have pushed him away the moment his hand touched her face. But she had been weak, and she hated herself for it. She didn't dare examine her feelings toward him. All she knew, was that there were many feelings she housed toward him. Anger, vexation, resentment... and an array of other things she couldn't name.

"You may be a fool, but at least you will be a fool who is also a marchioness," her mother said in a gleeful voice.

Jane squeezed her eyes shut, trying to drown out her mother's voice and the chaotic thoughts that racked her brain. Jane knew that simply disappearing from the ball with Lord Seaford would cause a stir among the crowd, but not enough to ruin her reputation, and only her mother had witnessed their kiss. The threat of 'gossip' spreading about the scene in the music room could come only from her mother.

"My reputation is not ruined, Mama. If you keep what you witnessed a secret, then—"

"I will do no such thing. If I did you would not be marrying Lord Seaford."

"I do not wish to marry Lord Seaford!"

"Nonsense. Do you hear yourself? To toss aside this opportunity would be to toss aside a fortune! A comfortable and prosperous living!"

Jane turned away. Her mother would never understand. She had come to Brighton for one reason: a chance to receive a proposal from Lord Barnet. The dream she had clung to for years had now been torn from her grasp at the hands of Lord Seaford and her mother. If only she had stayed in Ashford. She could have carried on dreaming, and perhaps Lord Barnet would have returned from Brighton in the spring unattached, and she could have taken her chance then. She would have never met Lord Seaford. Never laughed with him, never succumbed to a single one of his charming smiles, never kissed him.

Never married him.

She sat up, remembering Lady Tabitha, still at the ball and likely wondering where Jane had gone. Jane was a horrid companion. But did it matter now? She wouldn't be Lady Tabitha's companion for much longer. She would soon be married to Lady Tabitha's grandson—she would be a marchioness, the mistress of Pengrave. She tried to swallow but her throat was too dry. She recalled Lady Tabitha's sharp reminder from that evening. *Misfortune favors the wicked.*

Jane regretted every moment she had spent deceiving Lord Seaford into thinking she cared for him. She didn't.

Did she?

No. She didn't care for him at all. She repeated the words over and over in her mind until they seemed true.

Biting back her tears, Jane remained silent for the rest of the ride. Her mother rambled on about wedding preparations, and how impressive it was that Lord Seaford could acquire a special license for their marriage, and how surprised she was that Jane, of all her daughters, had managed to secure a match of such rank.

Jane breathed against the glass of the window, the chilled outside air leaving it frosted in fog. Listening to her mother speak, she wondered if she had ever been loved. Growing up, Jane had dreamed of finding someone that might love her, and who she could love in return. She had chosen Lord Barnet at a young age, replacing the reality that she was unwanted in her home with the dream that one day she would escape. One day she would fall in love and no longer be ridiculed by the people that should have loved her unconditionally.

Her mother's words reentered her comprehension. "Lord Seaford is a man of honor. He will marry you for your protection. This is the perfect outcome."

"I do not wish to marry for my protection, Mama," Jane said, her voice weak. "I wish to marry for love."

Jane's mother placed a hand on her knee. "You know how I value honesty, my dear. You have many talents, but I honestly do not believe any man could fall in love with you. You are twenty-two and have never attracted a proposal. It is not plausible. That is why this solution is so perfect."

Despite her effort to contain it, another tear slipped from Jane's eye as she stared at her reflection in the glass.

To win the love of her family based on her marriage would be worse than never winning their love at all. As she imagined her future, roaming the large halls of Pengrave, distant from her husband, resentment burning forever in her heart… she couldn't bear it.

"I suppose we will have to extend our stay in Brighton," her mother said. "I should hate to miss my eldest daughter's wedding, and I am sure Mr. Milton will share my opinion."

Jane knew her father would. He would be as pleased with her discontent as her mother. Perhaps Lady Tabitha would understand her pain. Surely Caroline would. Jane dreaded the day she would see Lord Seaford again. How could she face him after all that had transpired between them? How could she face him for the rest of her life?

It had been true that her fortune would turn this evening, but it did not turn in the direction she had hoped. Misfortune favors the wicked, indeed.

With a groan, Jane put her head in her hands, covering her ears against her mother's voice until they reached their destination.

Chapter 13

Turning in front of the looking glass in her bedchamber at Lady Tabitha's home, Jane studied the intricate detail of her wedding gown. Her mother had visited the town seamstress, paying much more than the dress was worth to have it finished within a week. Jane touched the lace on the sleeves, tracing the beaded embroidery with her finger.

Suzanne picked up a handful of pins, beginning on her hair arrangement. Jane stared, unblinking, at her reflection. She had not seen Lord Seaford since the day of the ball the week before. She had tried to avoid him, leaving the arrangements to be made between him and her mother. Despite the intention to keep the wedding a quiet affair, word had spread throughout Brighton and Seaford that the new marquess had already chosen a bride.

"I will miss you," Suzanne said from behind her, sniffing as she placed the pearl-studded pins in her curls. "I suppose you will have a new lady's maid at Pengrave."

Suzanne's farewell was only a sharp reminder of all Jane would be leaving behind. She would never live in Ashford again. She would see Caroline less often. She would rarely get to see and ride her horse, Locket. Her entire life had been changed.

She clasped Suzanne's hand in hers, locking eyes with her maid's reflection in the mirror. "You have been a dear friend to me, Suzanne. And I doubt I will ever find a maid so skilled at taming my hair."

Suzanne laughed, pulling her comb through a knot in Jane's hair, making her cringe. "It has been a pleasure to serve you, miss."

When Jane's hair had been styled and had earned her mother's approval, they removed to the carriage that would convey them to Pengrave. Lady Tabitha joined Jane and her parents in the carriage, giving Jane a look of pity. When Lady Tabitha had discovered what had happened in the music room, she had traveled alone to Pengrave in order to 'give her grandson the scolding he deserved.' Although upset with her grandson's behavior, she had still seemed pleased when informed of their pending marriage. It seemed Jane would be the only one opposed to it.

Her heart hammered the entire ride to Pengrave, nervousness fluttering in her stomach like a thousand frantic wings.

She reminded herself that simply because she would be married to Lord Seaford did not mean she had to interact with him often. She could request that he leave her alone. She could spend her days on the opposite side of the property, taking her meals at a different time than he did. She tried not to worry herself over the major details... such as the need to one day produce an heir. She pushed the thought from her mind as quickly as it came.

With her racing thoughts, she found that the ride passed much faster than it had the last time. She ignored her parents' remarks about the grandeur of the home as her father helped her down from the carriage. Jane's heart jumped to her throat as they entered the house.

Lord Seaford stood at the door of the drawing room, his eyes heavy and sullen, as if attending a funeral rather than his own wedding. She was shocked—she had never imagined that he could look so downtrodden. He was the liveliest person she had ever met.

He straightened his posture when her eyes met his.

She couldn't move as she studied the heaviness in his usually light and friendly brown eyes. She held her hands clasped together, wanting to look away from him but unable to. The raw pain in his expression disarmed the anger inside her, leaving her to sort through the other emotions that surged in her heart.

Jane followed her parents into the drawing room, passing Lord Seaford in silence. The awkwardness between them was tangible. The party Jane had traveled with to Pengrave would be the only guests for the brief ceremony.

Without wasting a moment, Jane and Lord Seaford were ushered forward by the priest sent to perform the marriage. She stared at Lord Seaford's cravat as the priest began speaking, willing her legs to stop shaking. They were married according to The Church of England Book of Common Prayer, and Jane could scarcely blink before the priest snapped his book closed, congratulating the new Lady Seaford.

Jane's mother embraced her, wiping tears from the corners of her eyes. The room spun in streaks of blurred color, and for a moment Jane thought she might faint.

"We leave for Ashford this afternoon," her mother said. "I hope you and your husband will visit us there soon."

Her husband? Jane stole a glance at Lord Seaford. Referring to him as her husband would take a long time to make sense in her mind.

Jane thought of her home in Ashford once again. She would miss her mischievous brother, Harry, even if he did have a propensity to throw ham at her face. Harry was staying at her sister Cecily's home during her parents' stay in Brighton. Though Jane missed him, she was glad he was not there to make her wedding more embarrassing and awkward than it already was. Jane had always hoped that her wedding would be bright and happy and beautiful, a celebration of love and devotion.

The sharp contrast of reality struck her heart like a heavy stone.

Jane's parents lingered in the drawing room for an hour, mingling with Lord Seaford and Lady Tabitha. Jane stayed on the opposite side of the room. What would she say to Lord Seaford once the company dispersed? A thousand ideas had crossed her mind in the week she had spent seething over his actions. She had planned dozens of harsh words, but the moment she had seen him in the entry hall that day, seen the pain and regret in his eyes, her anger had dissipated. All she felt now was a gnawing emptiness.

Jane's stomach clenched in dread as her parents bid her a final farewell. Jane followed them outside, begging her father with her eyes to stay a moment longer. She wasn't ready to be alone with her new husband. Her heart leapt as she saw Lord Seaford following the group from behind her as they walked down the steps of the front entrance.

She wrapped her arms around herself to keep warm, the cold breeze pulling at her intricate hair arrangement. She watched as her parents and Lady Tabitha climbed into the carriage, and to her surprise, Jane felt the threat of tears in her throat. Were they truly leaving her here alone?

"Farewell, Jane! Farewell, Lord Seaford!" Her mother waved her gloved fingers at her as the carriage door closed. Jane's father waved from beside her, smiling with enthusiasm. Lady Tabitha did nothing, staring at Jane and her grandson with a look of condolence as the carriage rolled away.

Jane released a shaking breath as the carriage faded down the long road. A tear slipped from her eye but she wiped it away before Lord Seaford could notice.

The sound of his boots reached her ears, crunching over the fallen leaves behind her. She sniffed. Crossing her arms more tightly, she could feel her heart jumping around in her chest like a wild horse. After several seconds, the silence between them became unbearable. She couldn't turn and have him see that she had been crying. She doubted she could even speak around the knot in her throat.

"Miss Milton," Lord Seaford began in a quiet voice.

Jane wiped the moisture from her cheeks. "I am not Miss Milton any longer."

Another crunch of the leaves told her he had moved closer. She shivered as a fresh wave of cool air whipped at her skirts. She stared ahead at the deserted road.

"I know what it is to lose your name by no decision of your own. I know the loneliness it brings, and I am sorry for giving you the same fate."

Jane clenched her jaw.

He breathed out a sigh. "Please look at me." His voice cracked with emotion.

Jane steadied herself before turning around. The question that had been bothering her for the last week slipped past her lips. "Why did you kiss me?" she whispered. Resentment still burned in her heart, stirring up renewed feelings of anger.

When she dared to glance up at his face, she wished she hadn't. Never had she imagined to see the seriousness in his features, the heavy regret that lingered there. "It was selfish and brash of me to take advantage of you in such a way," he said. "I understand if you cannot accept my apology, but please know that I am sincerely sorry for what I have done." Lord Seaford spoke in a voice that she did not recognize. It was cold, detached, and grim. "I should not have kissed you. That was far outside my bounds, and now you are required to suffer for it. No one should be forced to marry a person they do not care for." He looked away from her eyes, kicking away a leaf at his feet.

Jane studied his face, unsettled by the scowl in his brow and the firmness in his eyes. "Are you going to call me Lady Seaford?"

He looked up. "If you wish."

She shook her head. "I wish to be called Jane. My mother calls my father Mr. Milton and I have always despised it." She patterned her voice after Lord Seaford's, stern and business-like.

He gave a swift nod. "Very well. I shall call you Jane."

She eyed his mouth—the unyielding stiffness of it, and the lack of creases around his eyes. She didn't think she could ever miss a smile so much. "And what shall I call you?"

His eyes locked on hers, and for a moment Jane could see herself reflected in them. "Philip," he said.

She looked down, banishing the last of her wayward emotions. There was nothing she could do to change her circumstances now. She was married to *Philip,* she was mistress of Pengrave, and she would never reclaim the life she had once had. She would never have another chance to marry Lord Barnet. Her heart pinched with melancholy, but it faded. The loss of Lord Barnet felt like the time Caroline had lost her puppy as a child. It had been devastating to Jane for a moment, but she had recovered quickly. The puppy had not been *hers* to mourn. It had never been hers.

"*Lord Seaford* is still a stranger to me," Philip said. "We need not be strangers to one another. Only to society."

Jane thought she heard a hint of lightness in his voice, but his eyes remained the same, heavy and full of hurt. Shame scratched over her skin as she remembered the words she had spoken to her mother in the music room. She had spoken, without reserve, of her opposition to a marriage with Philip. She had failed to notice then how much those words had hurt him.

"You must be cold," he said in a quiet voice. "Come inside." He extended his arm to her.

Jane took it reluctantly, crossing the grass with her new husband. Warmth from the fireplace flooded through her as they entered the house. There would be much to explore within the walls of Pengrave and on the vast property. How could Jane ever become bored with so much at her disposal? She had mentally prepared herself for a lonely life, but within the pages of a book she could find many friends. The stables were full of horses that she could befriend as well. She would keep her distance from

Philip and still find a fulfilling and happy life. Her eyes slid to him and she released his arm.

"Shall we sit by the fire?" Philip asked.

Jane could think of nothing more uncomfortable than sitting with Philip, forcing polite conversation. She wrung her hands together. "I would rather spend the day alone in my chambers."

He nodded, looking down at the ground. "I will have a fire started in your room, and your bed is already prepared. I will fetch your maid to direct you there."

Without another word, Philip walked toward the staircase, his long legs carrying him up and out of sight in little time at all. Jane released the breath she had been holding, the tension in the room finally dispersing. Tomorrow she would explore the estate. The dark, mysterious aura of the house was exciting upon visiting, but living within the place was a different matter entirely. She would need to brighten it, if only to lift her spirits. And Philip's.

She had hardly been able to tolerate his friendliness, but this grim, brooding disposition did not suit him. The brooding characteristic had only flattered Lord Barnet. She knew she was to blame for Philip's pain, but she did not know how to remedy it.

Without permission, her thoughts traveled back to the music room of Clemsworth, the way she had felt in Philip's arms, the taste of spiced cider on his lips, and the way he had stolen her breath with his kiss. She banished her thoughts, appalled at herself. That kiss had been the most unfortunate event of her life; it was not a reverie. Jane's cheeks burned hot at the centers as Philip appeared at the top of the staircase, followed by a young maid with dark hair.

"Your room is prepared," he said in a curt voice.

"Thank you." Lifting her skirts, she climbed the stairs,

passing her husband without another sound. He looked down at her as she passed, and she met his eyes one last time before following her new maid to the top of the staircase.

Chapter 14

"I thought you becoming a marquess was surprising enough." Adam Claridge, Philip's most trustworthy friend, shook his head in shock.

"As did I," Philip said in a quiet voice.

Adam threw a look of dismay to his wife Amelia. They sat facing Philip on the settee of their drawing room in Brighton. The two had been married that summer.

Amelia studied Philip with intense focus, her brown eyes inquisitive and unblinking. A slow smile pulled on her lips. "You took advice from *Lord Ramsbury?*"

Philip rubbed his eyes. He hadn't been sleeping well of late, tormented by his own stupidity and the woman that slept in the adjoining chamber just beyond his door. It had been a fortnight since their wedding, and in those weeks Philip had hardly seen Jane at all. He had invited her to dine with him the first three days but had given up when she had insisted upon taking her meals alone.

He often heard her singing in the early morning, quietly from within her side of their chambers. Each morning he listened, remembering one of the many reasons she had first stolen his heart. They had passed one another in the hall outside the library once, and the awkwardness had been excruciating. He was sure that she hated him. How could she not?

"Yes, I took advice from Ramsbury," Philip groaned. "I did not intend to. But it was only a simple kiss."

"One must never underestimate the consequence of a simple kiss," Amelia said.

He shrugged. "Lord Ramsbury believes that if he had only kissed you that you would have fallen in love with him."

Amelia's eyebrows rose and she laughed. "Did you tell him he was wrong to believe that?"

Philip frowned. "No, I'm afraid not. I severely doubt he would have listened to me. He has the confidence of a thousand men."

"Arrogance is a more accurate term," Adam grumbled.

Amelia laughed, rotating on the settee toward her husband. "Are you still jealous of Lord Ramsbury? I told you his attempts to woo me were always in vain."

Adam planted a quick kiss on Amelia's cheek, and she stared up at him with such adoration that Philip found himself stricken with envy of his own. He would never have the joyful marriage that the Claridges shared. How could Jane ever love him after what he had done?

"Please enlighten me," Adam said, his blue eyes wide as he turned to face Philip. "Why did you consider for a moment that listening to *Lord Ramsbury's* advice was a wise decision?"

Philip threw his hands in the air. "He is so… convincing! But you must know, I was determined to ignore his advice until…" Philip paused. He did not wish to disclose every detail of his kiss with Jane.

Adam raised his eyebrows for him to continue.

"I do not need to elaborate," he snapped. He couldn't recall every detail himself, and to speak of that moment in the music room felt a betrayal to Jane. The memory sickened him with shame and regret, and to speak of it now would only intensify those emotions… and the longing he felt to kiss her again. *Blast it.*

Adam was far too amused with Philip's plight, sitting back on the settee with a grin.

Philip covered his face, blowing out a long puff of air through his fingers. "I do not know what to do. I have ruined her life. I have stolen her freedom and she detests me for it."

Adam's voice cut through Philip's self-pity. "You always told me that if a woman ever stole your heart, you would steal hers before another man could take the chance."

Philip dropped his hands. "I tried."

"Indeed, you did," Adam said with a chuckle.

"There is nothing more I can do."

"Why not?"

Philip puzzled over those words. "How can I turn her hatred into love? My opportunity to win her over has passed."

Adam rubbed his jaw. "What else did you once say to me… oh, yes. 'If you fancy her, devil take it, you pursue her!'"

Amelia covered her mouth, hiding her laugh.

Philip squeezed his eyes shut. He should have known his own words would be used against him one day. Why was it that advice was much easier to bestow than to follow?

"Your opportunity has not passed," Adam said. "It has only just begun. You live within the same walls as her now. You have years ahead to steal her heart."

"You must begin with simple things," Amelia added. "You mustn't overwhelm her, especially if she doesn't wish to see you."

"Simple things," Philip repeated.

"Yes. Write her a note, give her flowers, or invite her to accompany you to town. Do not pester her with endless apologies and flattery. You must show her that you can be trusted, that you care for her, and that you are her friend." Amelia smiled encouragingly. "You must come to know her. Come to know her interests, her strengths, her joys. Become her confidant and her friend before you fret about winning her heart."

Adam nodded. "I have never met a man more natural to befriend than you, Philip."

"You must be yourself," Amelia said. "You must learn to work together before you allow yourselves to be apart. The more distant you become from one another the more difficult it will be to change."

Philip sighed. He didn't know if it was possible for them to grow more distant than they already were. "But she does not wish to work together."

"Do you ever make an effort to see her?" Amelia asked.

He paused. "No, I suppose not. I fear she would push me away." Philip still felt the destructive effects that her words in the music room had placed on his heart. She had seemed repulsed at the notion of marrying him, acting as if she would rather die than spend her life with him. He had suspected that she had developed feelings for the Viscount of Barnet, but Philip had still hoped that she could choose him instead. He had been vastly mistaken.

"In your efforts to befriend her and gain her forgiveness, you must not dwell on the things that might go wrong," Amelia said. "Place your focus on the things that might go *right*."

Philip wished he had a quill and parchment with which to take note of Amelia's words. Her brown eyes sparked with knowledge and wisdom, and he knew he should heed her advice. Why had he not come to the Claridges before? Why had he run to Lord Ramsbury for advice? He had been so foolish. A complete niddicock.

The night he had kissed Jane in the music room, after she had fled with her mother, Philip had found Lord Ramsbury in the dining room. Dazed and drunk, he had laughed endlessly at Philip's plight. Something told Philip that Lord Ramsbury would have laughed even if he had been alert.

"Now." Adam pulled him from his thoughts, sitting forward. "You are to go back to Pengrave and remedy this situation as best as you are able."

Philip rubbed the back of his neck, his legs stiff and unmoving. His heart beat fast, echoing in his ears and weakening his resolve.

Adam pointed a finger at the door, laughter brimming in his eyes. "Go!"

Philip threw him a half-hearted glare before dropping his head with a smile. Both men felt the reminiscence of Adam's command. Just a few months before Adam had been too afraid to propose to Amelia. He had come to Philip's home in Brighton and Philip had demanded the very same thing to his friend.

Not only was Philip a niddicock, but he was a hypocrite as well.

Amelia raised her own index finger at the door, giving Philip a heartfelt smile. "Do not waste a moment."

Philip took a heavy breath, his chest quaking as he exhaled. Why was he so nervous? He was more nervous now than he had been the morning Jane had come riding at his estate. What if she rejected him again? What if she told him again how much she regretted that she was forced to be his wife?

He stood up, unable to resist the sharp gazes of his friends any longer.

Adam chuckled. "She will see you for the extraordinary man that you are, Philip. Give her time. Eventually she will see past your folly."

"Eventually." Philip's voice came out bleak. How long was *eventually*? He tried to bolster up his courage and optimism, but the effort was futile.

Making his way to the door, he ignored the whispers and laughter from the Claridges. They found far too much pleasure in teasing him. He threw them a half-hearted glare from the doorway of the sitting room.

"When you do manage to gain her forgiveness," Amelia said, "I would like to meet your wife. If she ever tires of your company and would like a friend, send her here to Brighton."

Philip gave a hard laugh. "Yes, so you may gossip about me."

She shook her head. "Only so I may talk a bit of sense into her in your behalf."

Philip threw her a smile of gratitude. After bidding them farewell, he entered the carriage that would convey him back to Pengrave. The weather had been too severe to ride his horse there, though he preferred that method of travel. The cold rain had begun early that morning and had only stopped for a moment before he had decided to pay the Claridges a visit. He had spoken through the door that connected his bedchamber to Jane's, telling her that he would be away for a short time. After a long moment of silence, she had replied with a curt, 'very well.'

The rain had begun to fall once again, mingling with the wind, splattering his carriage window. He scoured his mind for an idea on his way back to Pengrave, but he came up with nothing. Gaining Jane's affection felt more unlikely than the rain turning to brandy. He recalled Amelia's advice to simply be Jane's friend. First and foremost.

He would ignore his feelings, his own heartbreak, and focus his attention on making her happy, and showing her that he could be trusted.

The moment he returned home, he made a list on a sheet of parchment of all the things he could do for Jane. Simple things, just as Amelia had suggested. When he finished, he readied a second piece of parchment, scrawling a note that would be delivered the next morning. He planned to slip it under Jane's door before she awoke.

Jane,

It came to my attention that you may be finding yourself with little to occupy your time here at Pengrave. I will be spending today in town in search of a violin instructor for you. I know how you love the instrument. I hope it will provide you with the joy you deserve.

Sincerely,

Philip

He stared at the note, at the plain, business-like tone of it. He threw aside his worries, creasing the parchment and setting it on his desk. He sat back in his chair with a long exhale, threading his fingers behind his neck. Now, all he needed to do was find a violin instructor. He sat anxiously, considering going back into the rain to solicit his need in town, but the weather showed no sign of relenting. All he could do was wait.

Chapter 15

As he had feared, Philip awoke to rain again the next morning. Despite the weather, he dressed quickly, not waiting for his valet. After slipping his note under the door that separated his chamber from Jane's, he left the house on horseback.

Seaford was a small town, but the center held a prosperous market of many shops, booths, and solicitations. Unaccustomed to his abundance of servants, Philip hadn't thought to enlist one of them to seek an instructor for him. He wanted this gift to Jane to come solely from himself.

He spent an hour walking the streets of town, soaking himself with the rain, requesting brief audiences with several people that passed. One woman directed him to a nearby shop, one selling hand painted instruments. On the door, soaked and barely legible, was an advertisement that read:

*On moderate Terms,
The violin, piano forte, and singing,
Taught by Miss St. Clair
12 Rathbone Place*

Philip memorized the address and found the house within thirty minutes. Miss St. Clair answered the door, shocked to see the dripping wet Marquess of Seaford standing on her steps. She invited him inside, where she agreed wholeheartedly to teach Jane the violin beginning the next week.

After thanking her and counting himself fortunate, he mounted his horse and set off toward Pengrave. The estate came into view, blurred behind the sheet of rain that fell harder now. By the time he stepped into the house, he was soaked, especially his hair, sending droplets cascading down his face and drenching his jacket.

Philip's butler, Ambrose, stifled a laugh before turning it into a polite cough.

"My entire existence is a catastrophe, Ambrose," Philip said. "I do not need you to remind me of that unfortunate fact."

Ambrose cleared his throat, suppressing a smile as Philip blinked away the water that dripped into his eyes. "My apologies."

"But," Philip held up a finger. "I managed to find a violin instructor for Jane. Do you know where she is?" Philip asked in a quiet voice. Sound traveled easily within the walls of Pengrave.. "I must see her."

Ambrose shook his head. "I would advise you *not* to see her until you are dry and presentable."

"Do I not look becoming when I am soaked?" Philip asked, running his hand through his hair, the matted curls tangling between his fingers. He tugged, cringing in pain. Multiple strands of hair had wrapped and tangled around his hand, making it impossible to remove from his head. He lifted his other hand to untether his fingers, laughing at Ambrose's wide eyes.

"My hand is stuck." Philip gave a hard tug, only intensifying the knots he had created in his hair. He had never wished for straight, tamable hair more than in that moment. "Devil take it," he mumbled through his laughter.

Ambrose chuckled, not offering any assistance. He, like the Claridges, took far too much pleasure in Philip's distress.

Philip turned, hoping that a new angle would allow him to withdraw his hand. His eyes caught on a movement from down the hall, a sweep of lavender skirts. He froze, gesturing for Ambrose to be silent.

A light humming reached his ears as he tried to hide himself behind his butler, making one last vain attempt at freeing his hand before Jane stepped into the entry hall. Unfortunately, Philip was at least four inches taller than Ambrose, not including the added height from Philip's knotted hair and tangled hand.

Over the top of the butler's balding head, Philip made eye contact with Jane. "Good day," he stammered.

Her blue eyes flew open wide when they shifted up to his head. Philip felt his face grow warmer as she stared at him. Her lips pinched together, and her chin quivered.

Blast it. He had made the woman cry.

To his surprise, a loud laugh burst out of her, the sound

bouncing and echoing off the domed ceiling. She covered her mouth, as if the sound had been a shock even to herself. Philip smiled, stepping out from behind Ambrose, who retreated slowly toward the door.

"It seems I have found myself in a quandary," Philip said, chuckling as his face cooled.

With fascination, Jane stared at his hand, tangled in his hair. Her smile grew, and a little laugh escaped her again. "How did this happen?"

He glanced up, focusing on his other hand as it tugged on one stubborn curl that entangled his thumb. "I am not certain. These sorts of embarrassing and unfortunate things happen to me often. If I took the time to analyze each one I would be a very busy man."

Jane took a tentative step forward. She pushed back a perfect carrot-hued ringlet from her forehead, examining Philip's head as she rose on her toes. "I see the problem. Come stand near the staircase."

"Why stand near the staircase...?" his voice trailed off as Jane took a step up the stairs, turning to face him again. A smile still hovered in her eyes, but it was hidden behind a tentative, timid facade. She motioned for him to stand in front of her.

When he reached her, he found that her place on the step brought her to his height, her face level with his. She was so close. He could smell her rose perfume. He had only been this close to her once before, and it had been too dim to clearly see the details of her face. But he could see them now. A trail of freckles crossed from her right cheek to her left, tracing over the bridge of her nose. Her rosy lips pressed together in focus, creasing her cheek with a light dimple. And her eyes, narrowed in focus, held streaks of gray among the blue.

His breath caught in his throat as her gaze met his. She looked away fast. "Turn around, please. I am going to untangle your hand." Her voice had fallen into a serious tone, all traces of laughter gone.

He rotated on his heel, breathing in the silence as Jane touched his hand.

"I received your note this morning," she said.

"I found you a violin instructor." His voice was too boisterous. He cleared his throat. "She will begin your lessons next week."

"Thank you," she said after a long pause. "That was very... thoughtful of you." Jane's small fingers worked quickly, pulling on his hair without mercy.

"Do not thank me. I was simply sparing myself the horror of hearing you attempt to play the instrument again without instruction."

She tugged on his hair harder.

"Jane!" he cried through a laugh.

"Philip! Be still! Do you wish to have your hand attached to your head for the rest of your life?"

He had a feeling she was hurting him intentionally. Did he deserve it? Probably. But the sound of his Christian name in her voice was worth the pain. He ducked his head away before realizing that his hand had been freed.

When he turned around, Jane stood with her hands on her hips, one eyebrow raised. The front of her dress was wet from his hair. He flexed his fingers, giving her a grateful smile. She pressed her lips together again, hiding the smile he so wished to see.

"Thank you. You did not need to do that for me. You could have derided me like Ambrose." Philip turned to the door but found that the butler was gone.

"It was nothing. It is a wife's responsibility to keep her

husband from doing daft things and remedying them when he does."

Philip scoffed. "I have not heard that before."

"No, but I suspect that may be the way of our marriage," she said with a thoughtful expression.

His reaction was likely not what she expected. He threw his head back in laughter. "I will not argue with that point."

Jane watched him, that same thoughtful look still shrouding her pretty features. A roar of thunder cut the air, and Philip saw a flash of lightning reflect in Jane's pupils as she stared out the window behind him. "Storms are beautiful," she said in a quiet voice.

With great effort, Philip looked away from her face, glancing out the front window. The wind had calmed, letting the rain fall in consistent and straight paths from the sky. The water that covered the window put a shine over the darkness of the clouds. Another branch of lightning cracked the sky. "Indeed," he said.

When he was younger, Philip had imagined that the earth truly did crack when lightning struck, letting in the light of heaven for the briefest moment. He had always loved storms like this. If lightning truly was the light of heaven, then each strike meant another glimpse at his parents.

He realized how long and how wistfully he had been staring out the window. He looked over his shoulder at Jane and found that the storm still held her fascination as well. The silence between them was still fraught with misunderstanding and heartache. Philip wanted to reach up and touch her face, telling her once again how sorry he was. But what would that accomplish? Amelia had taught him the day before that he needed to *show* Jane how he felt. He already knew she doubted every word he spoke.

Her eyes shifted to his before she stepped backward up the stairs. "Do not touch your hair again," she said, turning around.

"Where are you going?" he asked in a careful voice.

She paused her ascent. "To my room."

"Do you not wish to see more of the estate? It is your home now. There is much about it I have yet to explore as well." Philip tried to keep his voice from sounding desperate. He waited as she considered the idea.

Jane stared down at him from her place on the stairs, a hint of confusion in her expression. She studied every feature of his face, as if she were trying to solve a puzzle. She was silent for a long moment before shaking her head, the movement so small he almost missed it. "Not today."

Before she could turn around again, he took a step up the stairs. The moment his right foot left the ground, his left lost balance, slipping in the puddle that had accumulated around his feet.

He grabbed the gold banister in an attempt to stop himself from falling, but still found himself on the ground within seconds, the puddle soaking into the back of his breeches.

All he could comprehend past his humiliation was the quiet laughter coming from the staircase in front of him. He fell into laughter of his own, putting his head in his hands before thinking better of it. With the luck of his day it was likely his hand would get stuck in his hair a second time. He didn't know if it was possible to embarrass himself further in front of Jane.

She walked tentatively down the stairs, lifting her skirts and watching for puddles. When she reached him, she extended her hand to help him stand. Laughter shook her small frame as he climbed to his feet. She must have thought he was ridiculous. The man she had wanted to marry instead, Lord Barnet, would never have been so ungainly.

Philip was certain that he was the most graceless marquess that had ever lived.

"Are you hurt?" she asked, her voice difficult to understand through her giggles.

"That depends on your definition of the word," Philip mumbled. He glanced at the seat of his breeches, cringing at the large, circular mark the water on the floor had made. Jane's laughter seemed to have become uncontrollable, and she hid her face behind her hands. The sound of her giggles only made him laugh harder—the sound being innately contagious.

"I am glad my shame brings you so much joy," Philip teased, gripping the banister and rubbing his boot over the floor.

Jane uncovered her face, her eyes wet with tears of mirth. Her laughter subsided, and she pressed down her smile. Her expression shifted, as if she were remembering something very important. "I must go."

"Where?" Philip asked, exasperated.

"To my room. I said it before." She started up the stairs, scowling over her shoulder as he began following her.

"Why?" He held the banister tightly, coming to a stop two stairs beneath her. She turned to face him, startled by his closeness. He retreated down a step. He did not want to scare her; he needed to tread carefully.

"Because I…" her eyes darted around. He had caught her in the midst of an excuse to avoid him. His heart stung but he ignored it.

"You do not have to tell me," he said in a soft voice. "I

understand if you don't wish to be near me."

Her cheeks reddened at the centers. "I—well—er—it sounds far to harsh when you say it in those terms."

"Is it true?"

"You said I did not have to answer your questions," Jane said, one eyebrow raised in defiance.

Philip laughed under his breath. He knew the answer was a resounding yes. An idea struck him. "Perhaps we might make a game of it."

Her brow furrowed. "A game?"

"Yes, a game, one that requires the opposite of what I said before." Philip searched for the correct way to arrange the words that were scattering in his mind. "We have been married for a fortnight, yet I know little about you, a misfortune that is entirely my fault. In this game, we shall each be given… an allotment of questions to ask the other. We may ask one another any question we want, and we must provide an honest answer."

Philip's 'game' had been invented just as the words escaped his mouth. "And we are only allotted three questions per day," he added. This way he could have a reason to claim Jane's company more often.

She considered it for a long moment. "One."

"One question per day?"

With a nod, she crossed her arms. "And you have already asked yours."

Philip raised an eyebrow. "But you did not give me your answer." He watched as she shifted uncomfortably under his gaze. He had asked if it were true—that she didn't wish to be near him. But he did not want to waste his one question on something that he already knew.

"Not to worry," he said when she hesitated. "I will ask an easier one today."

Jane glanced at him from under her lashes. "What is it?"

He leaned against the banister, feigning deep thought. "If you do not wish to explore the estate with me, what is it that you would like to do today?"

"That is your question?" She sounded relieved, as if she had been expecting a much more difficult one.

"That is my question," he affirmed.

Her gaze moved over his shoulder, amazement burning within her blue eyes as she watched the storm. She hesitated for a long moment. "I would like to go outside in the rain."

Philip had not been expecting that response. He laughed, studying her features to decipher if she was indeed serious. "Do you desire to suffer my same misfortune?" he gestured at his clothing, still dripping onto the stairs. Glancing out the front window behind him, he saw the heavy sheets of rain that still fell upon the property.

"Yes."

Philip could hear the smile in her voice. He returned his gaze to her, and she met his eyes with excitement.

"You are serious," he said, astonished. Who was this woman he had married? He had never heard of an elegant young lady that enjoyed strolling out of doors in the rain.

She nodded, stepping past him, moving down the staircase. He followed, tilting his head in confusion as she seemed to bounce with delight. When she crossed the black and white checkered floor of the entry hall, she turned to face him, one hand on the door.

"Are you coming with me?" she asked. He couldn't tell by her tone whether she wanted him to or not.

Before he could convince himself otherwise, he gave a firm nod. "Lead the way, if you will."

She pulled on the door, and Philip held it open behind

them. Jane stood in the doorway for a moment. Philip hoped she had changed her mind. The rain fell in large droplets, not showing any sign of relenting. If it had been a warm summer rain Philip would not have given it any thought.

"Are you certain you don't wish to stay inside? The cold could make you ill."

Jane ignored him, taking her first step away from the warmth of the house. She walked down the steps.

Philip chuckled as her hair quickly became soaked like his, and she wrapped her arms around herself, laughing. He followed her to the grass, squinting as the cold water fell down his face. "Shall we go inside now?" he called over the sound of millions of heavy droplets as they hit the ground.

She twirled in a circle, tipping her face up to the clouds. "Not yet."

Philip couldn't erase the smile that had plastered itself on his face as he watched her, spinning and laughing as the cold rain nearly drowned her. He had suspected that the timid, aloof woman he had met at his grandmother's home weeks ago was not the true Jane. If this carefree, somewhat odd woman before him was the true Jane... then he could consider his heart officially surrendered.

Laughing, he threw his hands in the air and spun in a circle, imitating her as he closed his eyes, turning his face to the sky. He glanced at her and she laughed. Her entire frame shivered, and her teeth chattered as she tried to smile.

"Jane!" he exclaimed through his laughter. "We must go inside. You're shivering."

She finally relented. Without thinking, he placed his hand on the small of her back, intending to guide her toward the house. Her shoulder blades tightened, and she moved away, her smile falling with his touch. Oh, yes. Philip had forgotten how much he disgusted her.

Everything Jane did was a mystery to him. She glared at him one moment, avoiding him entirely, and at other moments seemed to enjoy his company. He thought of their kiss. He had been certain she had returned it for the briefest moment, but then had pushed him away. Is that how she would behave toward him forever? Every time he began to feel a sense of progress, would she push him away?

It seemed as though she had already made the choice not to love him.

Inside the warmth of the house, Jane faced Philip, a large puddle already forming at her feet. The wetness of her hair transformed it to a dark auburn, her pale eyes contrasting sharply with the color. She stared up at him, drops of water trapped in her lashes. Her cheeks were flushed pink with the cold, and Philip had to stop himself from gathering her into his arms and kissing her again. If she was going to be indifferent, why could fate have not given him a wife that he found unattractive and dull? He found Jane to be quite the opposite.

"You should change into dry clothing," Philip said. "I will have a fire prepared in the drawing room."

Jane pressed her lips together before speaking. "A fire is already lit in my chamber."

Philip's heart sank. "Oh. I see."

She gave him a small smile before picking up her soaked skirts from around her feet with one hand, sloshing toward the staircase.

"Jane," he said, stopping her. "You have forgotten to ask your question of me."

She gripped the banister, throwing him a curious look. "I did not forget."

"Well, then, what is your question?" Philip gave her an encouraging smile. His heart raced in his chest. What would she ask? Was he truly prepared to answer *any* question?

She stood, deep in thought, for several seconds. She opened her mouth to speak but closed it again, her features contorted in deep concentration. Glancing at him, her eyes carried a hint of doubt. "When my mother demanded that you marry me ... were you happy? Or were you disappointed?"

Philip's breath refused to come as he pondered her question. Why had he invented this deuced game? A hundred lies coursed through his mind, but he settled on the truth. He needed to gain her trust, and there was no point in deceiving her. "I was neither happy nor disappointed." His voice shook. "I was angry, and I was sad. I was angry at myself for risking your reputation, and for taking away your choice in the matter of your marriage. And I was sad because I saw the dread you felt at the prospect of marrying me. I knew you didn't care for me like you care for the Viscount of Barnet." He gave her a soft smile, hoping to bring a lightness to his confession.

Jane stared down at him from her place on the stairs, her expression firm and unreadable. Philip's heart ached when she did not deny his words. The silence that hovered between them grew too heavy to bear, so Philip cleared his throat. "Plan another question for tomorrow."

Jane nodded, tearing her gaze from his face and looking down at her feet.

"Will you join me for dinner this evening?" Philip asked.

Jane's eyes flew back to his. He had not invited her to dinner for more than a week. She had given him no reason to believe that she welcomed his invitations. To his surprise, however, she said, "I will."

Philip couldn't stop his smile as Jane turned around and ascended the stairs, a trail of water following behind her. He wanted to follow to ensure she did not slip, but he thought it best to leave her alone. When he was sure she had reached the second floor, he jumped into the air, his enthusiasm uncontainable. As he spun around, he found Ambrose emerging from the drawing room, his blue eyes twinkling with amusement.

Philip gaped at him. "Have you been listening this entire time?"

Ambrose's eyebrows rose, the wrinkles in his forehead deepening. "Of course not."

Eyeing him with suspicion, Philip crossed his arms. Ambrose's expression was far too innocent. It was a complete act, Philip was certain. "What do you have to say about what you may have overheard?"

Ambrose gave a small smile that reminded Philip of his grandmother. The elderly seemed to have their own variety of smiles, used to convey their wisdom without boasting of it. "I would gather that you are making progress."

Philip bit his lip, raising his brows. "Truly?"

Ambrose nodded. "Any other woman might have run away at the sight of you soaked to the bone wearing your hand as an unwanted hat."

"You may be right." Philip laughed, pointing a knowing finger at his butler.

"I am always right," Ambrose said, straightening his jacket with a pompous smile.

Philip chuckled, slapping his butler on the shoulder

before setting off toward the staircase where he could change into dry clothing of his own, whistling as he went. His hope for the future had been heightened, spreading in his soul like the smile on his face. Perhaps his luck had finally turned.

As he reached the staircase he slipped, once again, landing hard in that same puddle.

Chapter 16

Rubbing the sleep from her eyes, Jane rolled to her side. A smile, uncalled for, pulled on her lips as she sat up in her bed. The moment she realized it was there she wiped it away, knowing the reason she was smiling. Philip, and all his endearing characteristics had somehow managed to coerce a smile from her even as she slept. How was that fair?

At dinner with Philip the night before, she had confessed her daily routine, and he had been both appalled and impressed. He made her commit to him that she would explore the property with him the next day, if only to escape the monotonous reading schedule she had adopted.

She didn't know why she had agreed to his game of questions. What would he ask her today? She both dreaded and looked forward to seeing Philip, the contradiction utterly confusing. Her heart fluttered but she ordered it to stop. She only had two hours before she would meet him at the back door of the house, and she would need to ensure her emotions were in check.

Jane had always been stubborn. Some had claimed it was the color of her hair that gave her that inborn trait, but Jane was certain it came from her mother.

Jane's mother had been stubborn enough to force Jane into this marriage, and Jane was trying to be stubborn enough to show how much she hated it. She had done well the first two weeks, keeping to herself and avoiding her husband. It had worked in her favor until the day before when Philip had been in the entry hall, flaunting his maddening smile with his hand entangled in his hair. Why had she offered to help him? She couldn't say. But she had been awfully lonely since their wedding, and she had become weak in her resolve to avoid him.

Pengrave was larger than even she had imagined. As she had wandered the house over the last two weeks, she had discovered many fascinating rooms. Three stories high, she had still failed to see each one. Most of the rooms on the upper floor were dirty and dismal, the servants' attempts to restore the rooms to something grand still in progress. The weather had been growing colder, and Jane had yet to establish a habit of riding daily with the horses that now partially belonged to her. She missed her own horse.

Jane had smuggled a stack of books from the library to her room, where she spent most of her days. She studied mythology and poetry, while also reading novels, immersing herself in stories of faraway places and heroes and true love.

Philip's response to her question the day before still

haunted her. She had not denied that she cared for Lord Barnet, but she found that she thought of him less every day.

Her new maid, Sarah, was not quite as skilled as Suzanne, but she was quickly learning how to tame Jane's hair. After only thirty minutes, Jane was dressed in a simple cream dress, and her hair was styled in a secure twist.

Jane sat on her bed as Sarah left the room, staring at the door that connected Philip's room to hers. The door had never been opened. Jane often heard Philip inside his room, speaking to his valet, or heard the creaking of his bed frame as he shifted in his sleep.

A knock on the door made her jump. She scrambled to her feet. "Yes?" she choked.

"May I enter?" Philip's voice came clearly through the closed door.

She checked the looking glass on the wall beside her, ensuring that her hair had remained intact. She stopped herself. Why did she care?

"Yes, come in," she said.

The door opened slowly, the hinges creaking. His face appeared around the frame, his smile wide and cajoling. "I thought you might join me for breakfast before we explore the grounds."

She nodded, recovering from her surprise that he had finally opened that door. As he smiled at her, stepping into the room, it was as if a barrier between them had been lifted—and it quite literally had.

"I'm glad you agreed," he said. "The cook has prepared ham, and I do not think I can finish an entire pig on my own."

Jane laughed. "That never fails to remind me of my brother Harry. He fancies throwing it at my face."

Philip's eyes widened. "I hope you do not mean the entire pig."

"No! Of course not," she said through her laughter. "Although that is likely his next plan of attack."

Philip grinned down at her, and she watched the shaking of his shoulders as he laughed. Since the day before, she had found it detrimental to look at his eyes. Deep brown, framed in dark lashes, Jane did not like the effect his eyes had begun to have on her, especially when they widened in his endearing and standard look of surprise.

"Please remind me not to have ham prepared if your family comes to visit," Philip said with a chuckle. He gave a look of mock consideration. "Or perhaps I shall, simply to provide our guests with a bit of dinner entertainment."

Jane gasped. "You wouldn't do that."

"I would."

"You are so vexing!" she said. Her cheeks immediately caught fire, remembering that those were nearly identical to the words she had spoken before he had kissed her in the music room.

Philip's smile did not falter for a moment as he stared down at her, sparing her the embarrassment of her misstep. It seemed he would never take offense to the insult.

"Knowing how much you enjoy being out of doors…" Philip threw her a pointed look, "I thought we might take our meal outside. It is a lovely day, and I recently saw the gardens from my window. They are beautiful this time of year."

Jane glanced outside. The sun shone through the drapes, leaving no sign of the rain from the day before. "Very well."

After finding her warmest cloak, Jane let Philip guide her to the gardens where a servant already awaited them with a large platter of bread, fruit, eggs, and of course, ham. Philip had been correct in saying that the gardens were beautiful. The trees still held most of their leaves, displaying every shade of color between red and yellow.

Philip set the tray on the grass before sitting down beneath a tree. "The ground is dry," he said with a smile, patting the space beside him.

Jane tentatively stepped forward, taking a seat on the grass. She tucked her skirts around her feet, touching the ground with one finger. "It still feels damp."

Philip gave her a look of amusement. "You are truly opposed to sitting on the slightly damp grass after you willingly ran outside in a storm?"

"I'm not opposed to it. I was simply making an observation," she said.

"May I make an observation?" Philip asked, leaning back on his hand.

She raised her eyebrows for him to continue.

"Your hair matches the leaves." He smiled, picking up a dry orange leaf from the ground and holding it up to her head.

She looked down. Her hair had always been her most memorable feature to those around her, and she hated it. The day she had come riding at Pengrave with Philip she had not cared what he thought of her hair, but now she felt differently on the subject. Did he mean to mock her by comparing her hair to the leaves? Her cheeks burned. "And are you opposed to it?" she asked, daring a look at his face.

The look in his eyes unnerved her, the admiration unmistakable. "Not in the slightest." His gaze focused on a curl that had fallen over her forehead. His hand lifted from the grass as if to brush it away. She froze, her heart jumping in her chest like a wild thing. He seemed to change his mind, scratching his knee instead. Disappointment dropped through her but she refused to acknowledge the reason.

Philip gestured at the platter as a distraction. "You must try the scones. The cook of Pengrave is truly the best I have ever had. That is one of the only reasons I no longer despise my life here at Pengrave."

Jane eyed the scones, shining with warm butter under the morning sun. "What are the other reasons?" she asked as she took the scone Philip offered her. She tried to sound nonchalant, but she was genuinely curious.

He glanced up from the platter, one eyebrow raised. "Is that your one question?"

She scoffed, feigning deep interest in the scone she held. "How are we to have a conversation at all if we are only allowed to ask the other *one* question."

"It *was* your idea," he said with a chuckle.

"Yes, but I meant only one *difficult* question."

Philip rolled his eyes dramatically, throwing his head back. "How are we to determine if a question is difficult or not?" He gave her a teasing smile.

"If... it delves into personal matters, or if it requires a longer response than a simple yes or no."

"I see." Philip took a bite of his scone, his eyes lighting up like a child eating a sweet. "But I'm afraid I must confess your question does indeed delve into personal matters." Jane watched him, her curiosity growing as he looked down, a shy smile pulling at his mouth. "In truth, you are the reason." His eyes met hers, and Jane's heart nearly escaped her chest.

"Me?".

His expression wavered at her surprised response, but

he held her gaze. "Less than a month has passed since I was torn from my home, given a new identity, and sent to an unfamiliar place to live in solitude. You are the reason I am happy here at Pengrave, Jane. You make it easy for me to smile amid so much change and difficulty."

The sincerity in his voice plucked at her well-kept emotions. Philip wanted her there, even if she was uncertain if she wanted to be there herself. Had she ever been wanted before?

She realized she had been silent for too long, staring at the platter of food, avoiding his eyes. When she looked up, he smiled, the lightness returning to his expression. "Although… when I consider it further, these scones might be the primary reason."

Jane gave a small gasp before recognizing the teasing in his voice. "But you just said—"

"I said these scones are the reason I smile." Philip nodded, taking a large bite. She barely caught his smirk.

"You said I was the reason!" Jane didn't know why she felt the need to argue with him when he was clearly only denying his previous words to vex her.

"Did I?" he asked, leaning closer.

"Yes, you did." Jane turned herself toward him on the grass.

"I'm not certain I recall—"

Before she could stop herself, she took a piece of ham from her plate, flinging it at Philip. It struck him across the mouth, stopping his words.

She froze, covering her mouth with one hand as the ham fell into his lap. Philip's jaw dropped, his eyes shining with amusement. And revenge. He reached for a bundle of grapes, plucking each into a pile in his hand. Jane burst into laughter, scooting away from him as he began throwing them at her in a continuous attack, the grapes bouncing painlessly off her arms and torso. Philip gave a wicked laugh, reaching for a slice of ham. She shrieked, pushing herself to her feet.

He fell to his side, reaching for the hem of her gown. "Wait!" His laughter came uncontrolled, much like hers, as he stared up at her from the ground, clutching her skirt like a child. "Don't leave."

"Will you promise not to throw ham at me?" she asked, laughing at the way he struggled for breath as he laughed. His laugh was one of the most infectious she had ever heard, and the expressions of his face contributed to the humor.

"*You* threw ham at *my* face!" he said.

She placed a hand on her aching stomach as she sat down, blinking tears from her eyes as her laughter subsided. "I do not know what came over me."

"You are becoming just like your brother Harry, I would imagine." Philip leaned onto his side, resting his head on his elbow.

"You are more like Harry than I am," Jane said. "I suspect he would love you very much."

Philip smiled. "Ah. So you and Harry *are* very much alike."

"Yes," Jane said, popping a grape in her mouth. Her eyes widened when she saw Philip's grin, realizing what she had just agreed with. "I mean—no. Well… we are alike in some ways." Her cheeks burned.

Philip studied her face, making her shift uncomfortably. She didn't understand why his opinion of her suddenly mattered, or why his brown eyes and unrelenting smile did strange things to her heart, threatening her composure. But the notion that she loved him? It was preposterous.

"In what ways are you alike?" he asked.

Relief flooded through her. At least he hadn't asked her to explain why she had denied that she 'loved him very much.' "Is that your question?"

Philip tapped his chin. "Does it delve into personal matters?" he asked with a smile.

"Yes."

He nodded for her to proceed. Without thinking, she relaxed her posture, leaning back on both her elbows, staring straight up at the cloudless sky. "Harry and I are both the oddities of our family," she said. "Harry is the youngest child, the only son, and the only child with a propensity for mischief."

"Are you certain he is the only one?" Philip asked.

Jane threw him a pointed look, making him laugh. He turned his head to look at her. His eyes shone with deep interest as she spoke. She returned her gaze to the sky, finding it difficult to focus with Philip so watchful and so near. She dropped her arms, settling her head down into the grass. She didn't know why she felt so comfortable beside Philip, enough to lay down under a tree like she used to do when she was alone at her home in Ashford. A crow flew above them, landing in a distant tree on the property.

"I am the eldest child and have always been the most overlooked. I have three sisters, all of which my mother flaunted at social events, introducing them to every potential suitor and influential acquaintance, while I was instructed to wait at the outskirts of the room with my father. Harry and I, the eldest and the youngest, have simply been... the plain packaging for my parents' treasured middle children." Jane raised three fingers into the air as she named them. "Cecily, Emma, and Abigail."

Speaking the words aloud made her chest pinch with sadness. It wasn't the feeling of fresh grief, but the lingering ache of a distant sorrow. She had accepted long ago how unwanted she was. She turned her head to the side where Philip still faced her.

His brow furrowed, a certain frustration in his gaze. "I don't understand."

"What is there to misunderstand?" Jane asked with a laugh, though she didn't feel it.

"I don't understand how you could possibly be overlooked. You are intelligent, and you are a talented singer and rider. And an accomplished violinist!" The passion behind his words led him to sit up, hovering over her where she lay reclined on the grass.

She laughed at his reference to her horrendous violin playing. Emotion tightened in her throat, and tears burned in her eyes. She could excuse the tears for her laughter, but she knew they were born of the tender sincerity of Philip's words.

"You see! You have a lovely laugh as well!" He smiled down at her.

"That is enough," she said, calming her laughter. A tear had slipped from her eye, streaking down her temple and into her hair. She hoped Philip hadn't noticed.

He shook his head. "No. It is not enough. I will not stop until I know you can disregard what your parents have said. I will not stop until you understand how utterly magnificent you are." The frustration still lingered in his voice as he stared down at her.

Jane kept her mouth closed, fighting the emotion that tore through her. Her heart pounded so hard she worried Philip would hear it.

"What I have seen of you in the short time I have known

you is proof that you are nothing to be overlooked. Only a fool would do that. You are quick witted, humorous, and positively adorable. It takes just one look at your eyes to see that your character extends even deeper than what you reveal to strangers. Your smile could make any man forget his sorrows, and could even tempt him into an unwarranted kiss in a music room."

Jane gave a soft laugh, afraid it would turn into sobs as tears began falling freely down her temples. She didn't understand the emotions that choked her, and she didn't entirely believe the words Philip spoke, but they permeated her very soul with belonging and hope.

Philip's eyebrows fell in concern as he looked down at her. With deep concentration, he lifted one hand from the grass, catching her tears as they fell. She closed her eyes and her breath shuddered on the way out. His hand was cold, yet his touch filled her with warmth like she had never felt before. The contradiction confused her.

His hands smoothed back the hair that stuck to her wet cheeks, his movements slow and deliberate. "Please know that I will treasure you, Jane." He stared into her eyes. "Always."

His words settled in her heart like a precious gift. She watched his face, blurry behind her tears. She blinked, letting his features come into full focus. His clear brown eyes narrowed in concentration. His dark eyebrows, the unmistakable lines at his eyes and mouth from years of smiles, and the new stubble that had begun to grow on his cheeks and jaw. And then there was the crease of his forehead, the one that she didn't yet understand. Only one well acquainted with sorrow could have developed such a crease. Was there a time Philip frowned more that he smiled?

"But will you treasure me more than the scones?" she choked through her tears.

He smiled without reservation, brushing the back of his hand against her cheek before meeting her eyes. "I will have to thoroughly consider that question."

She laughed, sniffing back the last of her tears. She hated the fact that her parents were now so proud of her, but only because of the man above her. By no design of her own, she had pleased them, winning their favor through a mistake—marrying Philip. But was it truly a mistake? Years of neglect had taught her to defy her parents, disagreeing with them on every matter possible. They adored Philip, but only for his title and fortune.

Jane was beginning to adore him for many other reasons, none of which involved his wealth and social standing.

He was so close, his face less than a foot above her. Her heart thudded in her chest. If she had the courage, she could have reached up and brushed the dark curl away from his forehead and asked what had caused the troubling crease that rested there. But her question for today was spent, and her emotions were running too wildly for her to interpret them.

His eyes searched her face before settling on her mouth, a look of longing in his expression. Her heart leapt. Would he kiss her again? She thought of the impropriety of their position but remembered that he was her husband now. A second kiss could have no repercussions that had not already occurred. Could it? Her heart beat so hard it hurt, catching fire within her, igniting her with longing for Philip, for a kiss she should not have wanted. He slid one hand behind her neck, his other hand lifting slowly to her face. His fingers traced her cheek, her jaw, coming to a stop at her lips. She couldn't breathe as he took her chin in his hand, brushing his thumb across her lower lip.

A cool breeze rustled the leaves around her head, cutting through the silence that had fallen between them. Philip drew back, half his mouth lifting in a soft smile. His fingers dropped from her face and he pulled his hand out from her hair. A strange sense of disappointment fell through her, but she tried to ignore it.

Settling back onto the grass beside her, Philip propped his arm behind his head. After a long moment, he broke the awkward silence, turning his gaze toward her. "I could stay here all day."

She drew a deep breath, hoping the chilled air would cool the burning within her. "As could I." Her own words surprised her, but it was true. Despite the new and unsettling feelings that grew inside her, she felt comfortable, safe, and content with Philip. The weather was beautiful as well, a rare autumn warmth in the air.

Philip's eyes widened. "Truly?"

She shrugged. "It is a beautiful day." She focused her gaze on the sky.

"Shall we try it?" he asked, a smile evident in his voice.

"Try what?"

"Shall we try to spend the entire day in the gardens?"

Jane turned her gaze toward him. He did not appear to be jesting. "The entire day?"

He laughed. "You said you could spend the entire day here."

"Did I?" She feigned confusion.

"Yes!"

"Are you certain?" She rolled to face him, laughing at the frustration in his features. She was using his own method of teasing against him.

When he realized it, he burst into laughter, shaking a finger at her. "You're clever. I might add that to my list of your magnificent qualities."

Jane pressed her lips together, hiding her smile. "I would like to stay here all day. Because autumn is my favorite season, you know." She didn't fully understand why she felt the need to explain her reasoning for staying out here with him.

"It suits you," he said. "I would have guessed that."

"I would guess your favorite season is summer," she said.

He shook his head. "Spring."

"Why spring?"

"To understand why I love spring you must first know how much I despise winter," he said. An image of Philip wrapped in layers of jackets with large snowflakes entangled in his hair flashed in Jane's mind. She laughed. It made perfect sense that he would be averse to winter.

"I despise snow and ice," he said with a grimace. "As you already know, I am the most graceful man in all of England." He winked at her. "Ice has a way of sending my feet out from under me more often than I would like."

Jane couldn't stop her laughter. She had to agree that ice and Philip would not be compatible in the slightest.

"It is so dreary and cold. The trees are barren, the ground is solid, and there is scarcely any color to be seen." His gaze grew distant, his expression grim. "It will never fail to remind me of the worst time of my life."

Jane's breath caught at the grief in his eyes, heavy and broken. But the expression was fleeting, and his smile returned as if it had never left. "That is why I love spring. Each year it's as if the world is awakening from a terrible nightmare, a season of despair, brushing itself off and declaring that it will reclaim joy, avoid defeat, and begin anew." The passion in Philip's voice and face captivated Jane. "The flowers bloom and color is born again. The green grasses reappear as the snow melts, and the sky shines blue once more. The clouds part and reveal the sun—a light that was always there, but simply hiding, forgotten amid the winter storm."

Jane held her breath as she listened. He continued with his explanation, and by the time he finished, Jane had almost decided that she loved spring more than any other season as well.

In the hours that followed, their conversation carried on without pause. They spoke of light things, and Philip told her story after story of his travels around the continent earlier that year. She told him stories of her childhood, and they laughed until her stomach ached. Philip ordered their midday meal to be sent to the gardens as well, and when they had finished eating, they returned to the grass where Philip took to burying Jane in a blanket of leaves.

Exhausted from what felt like endless laughter, Jane eventually fell asleep there beside Philip on the grass, much like she had fallen asleep under the tree at her home in Ashford. Her eyes had been incapable of staying open for a moment longer.

What felt like only minutes later, she opened her eyes to an orange sky, streaked with the colors of sunset. It must have been late afternoon. She sat up fast, squinting in confusion at her surroundings, momentarily forgetting the events of the day. She was brought to quick recollection when she looked down to see Philip beside her, his head lolled to the side in deep slumber. She smiled at the way his face contorted against the arm he used as a pillow, the peaceful relaxation of his features, and the dark curls that fell over his forehead.

Careful not to disturb the crunchy leaves around her, she scooted closer, lifting her hand tentatively to clear the hair from his face. The sleeping Philip was so endearing, she couldn't bring herself to look away. Her breath hitched as she stared at him, the feelings in her heart unfamiliar and different from anything she had felt before.

Without warning, his eyes fluttered open. She looked away fast, her cheeks growing hot. He had caught her watching him sleep. He would tease her relentlessly for it. The moment his eyes found her, he smiled, pushing himself to a sitting position with a groan. "Good morning," he said, his voice hoarse.

Jane laughed, relieved that he had not seemed to notice her staring. He blinked, reaching for his pocket watch. "Evening is nearly upon us, which means we have accomplished our goal."

She didn't want to leave, even as the temperature dropped with the sun. She shivered, and Philip took note, eyeing her with concern. "Come now, let us go inside." He stood up, brushing the leaves from his breeches. Bending down he took her hands, pulling her to her feet, and they started in the direction of the house.

Her heart leapt as he smiled down at her, a shyness in his expression. "You have not been riding," he said as they passed the stables.

"It is not the same," she said with a sigh. "It is not nearly as enjoyable without my horse from Ashford."

"I thought we agreed my horses were superior?" he asked in a teasing voice.

Jane rolled her eyes. "I will always prefer Locket."

Philip was silent for a long moment as if contemplating a deep thought. "Will you ride with me in the morning?" he asked. "After your violin lesson, of course."

Jane nodded, ignoring the excitement that welled inside her. Why was she suddenly looking forward to seeing Philip? Never had she imagined such feelings would ever exist within her. What had happened to her plan? She had been determined to enjoy her life at Pengrave, but to enjoy it in solitude. She had never expected to find such a dear friend in her husband, and she had certainly not expected to feel such conflicting emotions toward him. She didn't know what to call the feelings in her heart, but she knew one thing for certain.

She would gladly spend another day with him.

They ate dinner together in the large dining room that night, and when evening fell, they walked to their chambers together, entering through separate doors. Jane closed hers behind her, leaning against the wall.

A smile tugged at her lips as Philip called out his second, "Good night," from his room.

Chapter 17

The next morning, Jane arose early for her first violin lesson. When her maid arrived to help her get ready, she told Jane that Philip already awaited her in the music room.

After she was dressed with her hair tamed, she hurried to the staircase, excitement pulsing through her. She had always wanted to learn to play the violin, and Philip's thoughtful gesture of finding her an instructor made the endeavor of learning the instrument even more alluring. She thought of the hours she would spend practicing her violin within the grand music room, with Philip listening and offering teasing critiques.

When Jane had first moved to Pengrave, she had been shocked with the grandeur of the music room. She wanted to learn every instrument.

On the third floor, Jane walked to the open doorway

of the music room, pausing when she saw who could only be her violin instructor, Miss St. Clair. Young and beautiful, she sat on the bench of the pianoforte, smiling at Philip. Her blonde hair bounced as she laughed at something he said.

A stab of inferiority dug into Jane's heart as she studied Miss St. Clair, taking note of Philip's friendly smile directed at her from behind the pianoforte.

Jane entered the room and Philip glanced up. As his eyes settled on her, his smile grew to an impossible size. He stepped around the pianoforte.

"I trust you slept well?" he asked, taking her hand in his. Jane eyed Miss St. Clair from around Philip's shoulder. Jane had not liked the way she had been flirting with Philip. Had he been flirting with her as well before Jane arrived?

Miss St. Clair had golden hair like Jane's sisters, bright eyes and a lovely smile. Jane's attempt to look beautiful that morning suddenly felt like a futile effort beside her violin instructor. Jane had been picturing a middle-aged woman, not a pretty young girl like Miss St. Clair.

"I did," she muttered in response to Philip's question, giving him a brief smile.

"What is wrong?" he asked in a quiet voice.

"Nothing."

He studied her face, one skeptical eyebrow raised. Eventually his expression smoothed over and he bent down to be closer to her height. "Miss St. Clair is a very accomplished violinist. You are going to learn quickly from her, I know it." His eyes hovered over Jane's forehead before he raised his hand to brush aside a curl. "You look beautiful," he whispered.

Jane pushed aside the feelings of doubt that stirred in her heart as Philip led her to stand beside her instructor.

Over the next hour, Jane felt every level of frustration as she attempted to play a simple scale. And her frustration grew as she watched the smiles Miss St. Clair threw at Philip from over her shoulder. Did she not realize that Philip was a married man? He was Jane's husband, not an eligible gentleman to be flirted with. When the lesson was over, Jane bid Miss St. Clair a curt farewell. Philip thanked her, his smile much too wide and friendly. Miss St. Clair's cheeks deepened to a cherry red as she exited the music room.

Why Jane had felt so threatened by Miss St. Clair's presence she did not understand, but jealousy burned on her cheeks. What was wrong with her?

She stood with her back to Philip. There was no way that he hadn't noticed her curt behavior toward Miss St. Clair. How would she explain it to him? She could hardly explain it to herself.

"Did you enjoy your lesson?" Philip asked from behind her. His voice held a hint of confusion. Clicking on the marble floor, Philip's boots stepped closer.

"Not nearly as much as Miss St. Clair enjoyed it," Jane grumbled. She clamped her mouth shut, eyes wide.

Philip took hold of her arm, his gentle grip turning her around to face him. "What did you say?" he asked, his eyes searching hers, shining with amusement.

"I said that it seemed to me that Miss St. Clair thoroughly enjoyed your company. And you too were quite friendly toward the woman that clearly found you attractive. One could very easily interpret your behavior as flirtatious." Jane looked at the floor as she spoke.

Philip gave a hard laugh of disbelief. "You are jealous."

Jane's eyes flew up to his. "I am not! I—I was simply making an observation."

His eyes sparked with amusement. He seemed far too pleased. "And this observation… are you opposed to it?" The conversation felt oddly familiar, reminding Jane of the morning before in the gardens.

"Are you admitting that you flirted with her?" she asked, planting her hands on her hips.

"No. I did not flirt with Miss St. Clair. But if I had, would you be opposed to it?" He laughed through his words, staring down at her with a broad smile.

"Well—I—" Jane stumbled for a response. "You are married to me. You cannot develop a habit of flirting with women that are not your wife. The public will deem you a rake."

He pressed his lips together, narrowing his eyes. "Is that the only reason?" His voice was light, but it carried a hint of deep curiosity, as if he truly cared to know.

Jane swallowed. "Yes. That is all."

Philip still stared at her with skepticism, but he didn't question her further. Jane didn't know why it was so difficult to admit that she cared for him. In the beginning, she had been so firm in her resolve never to love him. To admit that she was indeed falling in love with him would be like admitting defeat. And she was afraid. What if Philip changed his mind? What if he began to see her flaws like her family saw them?

"I am curious," Philip said, his brow furrowed. "What of my actions did you interpret as *flirting*?" As he said the word a smile tugged on his lips.

Jane shrugged. "You… you smiled at her. And you made her laugh."

Philip scoffed. "That is not flirting. I'm quite certain I am the most inexperienced man in the world when it comes to flirting. But," he paused, raising his eyebrows,

"I was once given instruction by a man among the most experienced."

"Who?"

"My friend, Lord Ramsbury, of course."

Jane rolled her eyes as she recalled the pompous man that she had briefly met in the assembly rooms with Lady Tabitha. It did not surprise her that he considered himself an expert in wooing women.

"Lord Ramsbury has a way with women ordinary men will never understand," Philip said with a teasing grin. "He understands what it means to charm a lady."

Jane crossed her arms. "You certainly charmed Miss St. Clair."

Philip blew out a long puff of air, tipping his head back. "That was not my intention …"

"If that was not real flirting, then what is?"

He threw his hands in the air. "I am not an expert, nor will I ever claim to be."

"Perhaps I might find Lord Ramsbury and ask him to demonstrate." She took a step toward the door.

"You wouldn't dare," Philip said with a chuckle. "He will be all too pleased to comply with your request."

Jane hid her smile, turning to face him again. "Would Lord Ramsbury's flirting with me make *you* jealous? Would you be opposed to it?" she raised one eyebrow.

He opened his mouth to speak but closed it again, as if debating over a series of possible responses. "No—er—I suppose I would be worried for your reputation. If the public witnessed Lady Seaford enraptured by the flirtations of Lord Ramsbury you would be ruined for certain."

"Is that all?" she asked.

Philip stared at her, his eyes narrowing. "Is that your question for today?"

"Perhaps."

Half his mouth lifted in a smile and he shook his head. "Then I suppose I must answer honestly. That is one of the rules, you know."

"Indeed."

Philip drew closer, tipping his head down to look at her. "No."

"No?" Jane's heart pounded.

His clear brown eyes gazed into hers, and for a moment Jane wondered if he could see her heart through them and decipher all the secrets it held in regard to him. His expression grew serious as his gaze roamed her face. He was so close. Jane could hardly breathe.

Captivated by his face, Jane hadn't seen him reach for her hand until she felt his touch, his strong fingers hooking around her own. She inhaled sharply, looking down as he lifted her hand level with his waist. He traced his thumb over the top of her knuckles, each movement sending chills cascading over her arms. She hoped he couldn't see them.

When he met her eyes again, he brought her hand to his lips, pressing a lingering kiss on top of it. Her breath caught in her throat and she felt the temperature rising in her cheeks and the tips of her ears.

Philip drew his lips away from her hand before bringing it to his chest, pressing it into his shirt. Jane felt the steady beat of his heart against her palm, his voice sending subtle vibrations through her arm. "I would certainly be opposed to Lord Ramsbury's flirting with you," he said, his voice low. A slow grin crept over his lips. "Because it would vastly outperform my own attempt."

Jane pushed against his chest with a gasp, stepping away from him. Her heart still raced, and her cheeks burned. He had been teasing her!

Philip laughed before offering a bow. "*That* was my attempt at charming you, Jane. Are you quite charmed?"

She shook her head, refusing to admit the effects that he had had on her. "Not in the slightest."

He gasped in false offense, pressing his hand to his chest in the place Jane's had just been. She shook away the memory of his heartbeat under her fingers, the warmth of his closeness and the touch of his lips. "I am acutely offended," he said, a smile breaking through his facade. "But I am not surprised. It will be the greatest challenge of my life to win your regard after what I did to lose it."

Jane studied his face, the teasing glint in his eye fading, lost behind the honesty of his words. She had almost forgotten the means by which they were married. It no longer felt like an obligation, like a curse or a misfortune. She felt a strong sense of belonging among Pengrave and especially beside Philip.

"May I ask my question now?" he asked.

Jane gave a reluctant nod.

Stepping into the space she had pushed him from, Philip stared down at her. "If you were given an opportunity to turn back time, to never have met me in Brighton, would you take it?"

Jane swallowed. Hope and fear mingled together in his eyes as he waited for her response.

"No," she said.

"No?" Philip's eyes widened in surprise.

Jane couldn't stop her smile. "No. If I did that then I would not have a riding partner for this morning."

He laughed, dropping his gaze. "That is a true statement."

Jane smiled up at him, memorizing every line and color of his face, the lopsided tilt of his smiling mouth and his curls. "Shall we go?" she asked. "I should like to ride Brimmer again. He has just the right level of spirit."

With a chuckle, Philip nodded. "If you insist."

After changing into her riding habit, Jane met Philip by the stables, where they began their ride with a race, and ended with a slow ride through the trees behind the property. They spent the rest of the day together as well, eventually returning to the music room where Philip watched Jane as she practiced her violin. Philip made an attempt at singing along, which made it nearly impossible for Jane to hold her bow amid her unrelenting laughter.

By evening, they settled by the fire in the drawing room, where Jane fell asleep in the wide armchair. She vaguely remembered two strong arms lifting her before she was encased in warm blankets, a soft pillow at her head. The click of a door was the last sound she heard before all consciousness fled.

Chapter 18

Philip greeted the next day with excitement. Jane had seemed to be enjoying herself in his company, and she had not been as distant as she had been in the past weeks. He was making progress, just as Ambrose had said.

And he was falling more in love with her with every second that passed, with every beat of his heart, and with every smile she cast his way. The last time Philip could remember being so happy was before his parents had passed away, before he had known true sorrow. Jane was like his long-awaited springtime, bringing true joy back to his life when he hadn't realized it was gone.

The day passed much like the one before, with perfect weather to match. After their morning ride, they found a new spot on the property, and Jane shared her favorite passages from some of the books she had been reading.

He kept his question simple that day, asking for her fondest memory. She relayed a story of her birthday, years before, when she had received her beloved horse. His heart pinched when he saw the sadness in her eyes, the longing for the animal he had forced her to leave behind.

After much begging, Jane agreed to sing a song for him. He demonstrated his novice skill on the pianoforte while she sang a breathtaking melody. Philip was secretly glad her parents had underestimated her accomplishments and beauty. Otherwise she would have surely been married years before, and he would have never known her.

Over the following week, Philip learned more about Jane each day, finally discovering the woman he had seen hiding behind the shy facade in his grandmother's drawing room. They took a ride together every morning before returning to the house for breakfast, eventually settling in the library or music room where they talked and laughed for hours, read and discussed literature, or simply sat together in peaceful silence. Philip had been neglecting his household duties, but his servants did not appear to mind when they saw him with Jane.

Since the day in the gardens, when he had nearly kissed her, Philip had determined to tread carefully. He would not kiss her, though he longed to. Every blush that crossed her cheeks, every smile that touched her lips tempted him. But their first kiss had been destructive, and he refused to ruin his progress by kissing her again. He was still uncertain of her feelings for him, and he was happy with their friendship.

He hoped one day she would come to love him, to build a marriage with him like his parents had shared, but each time the hope crossed his mind he pushed it away. The greater his hope, the harder his fall.

Patience had never been one of his virtues, and Jane was teaching him patience like he had never before known. But she was worth waiting for and fighting for. Even if it took years, Philip would never stop trying to win her heart.

He had never wanted anything so much.

By the end of the week, the weather grew colder, and the first flakes of snow began to fall, coating the grounds with a blanket of white. November had almost drawn to a close, and winter was upon them. Normally a season of dread, Philip felt nothing but joy. He had been planning a visit to his grandmother in Brighton, where he would also take Jane to meet the Claridges.

The morning of Jane's second violin lesson, Philip jumped out of bed. He shivered in the cold of the house. After dressing as quickly as he was able, he hurried to the door between their rooms. She usually arose around eight o'clock, and his clock read half past.

"Jane!" he called in a cheerful voice, knocking his fist lightly against the door. "Are you prepared for your violin lesson today?"

When he heard no response, he took a step back. Could she still be asleep? If so, his voice would have awoken her. He still felt strange opening the door between their chambers, as if he were invading her privacy in doing so.

He stared at the handle before trying to reach her with his voice one more time. "Jane, are you awake?"

Silence.

A feeling of dread thudded in his chest as he reached for the door handle. Something was wrong. He eased the door open, glancing at her bed. She lay beneath the covers, her eyes closed. He looked closer, fear settling over his shoulders when he noticed the paleness of her skin and lips, and the sheen of perspiration on her furrowed brow.

Rushing to her bedside, he gripped her shoulder, placing his other hand against her forehead. It burned with a fever. "Jane?"

She stirred but her eyes remained closed, her body shaking beneath the covers.

Philip's heart pounded with dread. He ran to her door, calling to a nearby maid to bring a bucket of cool water, and instructing another to call for the physician. He returned to her side, his own legs shaking as he studied her face. The color of her skin reminded him of a winter day, ten years before, when his mother had lay in her bed stricken with the illness that would soon claim her life.

"Jane," he said in a hoarse voice. He smoothed back her hair, the heat of her face radiating out to her hairline. His heart raced, and emotion tightened in his throat. He tried to calm his breathing, reminding himself that he could not conclude anything from her current condition. It could have been a minor fever, or a passing cold. He touched her cheek, hoping it would awaken her, but she remained unresponsive to his words and his touch.

The maid returned with the water and a damp towel. Philip plunged his hand into the bucket, ringing the excess water from the towel. He placed it on her forehead and the maid lifted the blankets from on top of her.

"We must keep her cool, Master Philip." The maid stared at Jane with deep concern. "The physician has been sent for."

He nodded, his throat too tight for words. The maid left the room and Philip took Jane's hand between both of his, afraid to blink as he watched her. The bright red of her hair contrasted sharply against her pale skin and the whiteness of the bedclothes. He touched her face, desperately hoping to find it cooler, but it still burned. Her body quaked with a shiver, and her brow twitched under the towel.

"Jane?" he whispered, smoothing his hand over her cheek. What had happened? The night before she had seemed perfectly well at dinner, and they had spent the evening together by the fireplace in the drawing room. They had ventured outside the morning before, but only for a brief walk. Fear gripped him with unrelenting hands as he stared at her, so small, laying in front of him, unalert and plagued with such an intense fever.

Painful memories coursed through Philip's mind like the blood in his veins, pulsing past his ears. He could still clearly imagine the sight of his beautiful mother, once so loud and joyous, frail and defeated beneath the white covers of her bed. And his father just weeks later, still broken from the loss of his beloved wife, suffering through the same illness that had claimed her, left with little worth living for. Only Philip. But it had not been enough. Philip had watched them both take their final breaths, one after the other. All he cared for in the world had been torn from his grasp. For ten years he had lived without them, but the pain still felt fresh and new.

Tears burned at his eyes as he held Jane's hand. Could life be so cruel as to take her from him too? He couldn't bear to imagine his desolate existence at Pengrave without her. Ten years had taught him how to pretend to be happy, but in a few short weeks Jane had taught him how to be truly happy once again. He couldn't lose her. He couldn't.

He kissed her hand, resting his head on top of it as he waited for the physician. Hot tears escaped his eyes, soaking into the blankets. He tried to calm his mind, but buried images and emotions and memories sneaked to the surface, stealing his composure.

What felt like hours later, the physician arrived, rushing through the doorway. He removed his spectacles, rubbing the frost from the lenses as he approached Jane's bedside.

Philip stood, giving the physician the needed space to examine her. "Good day, my lord. I am Dr. Fernside. I suspect this is Lady Seaford?" the physician asked, opening his case on Jane's bed.

Philip nodded, swallowing against his dry throat. "Are you able to help her?"

Dr. Fernside didn't seem to hear him, placing a hand against Jane's forehead. He scrawled something down on a sheet of parchment before pulling back one of her eyelids, leaning for a closer look. After listening to her heart, testing her pulse, and administering a series of tests, he finally addressed Philip again. "Just last night I saw a patient in Hove suffering from a similar condition."

Philip's heart dropped. "What is it?"

"I cannot be certain, but the symptoms are none that I haven't seen before. Great care must be taken to keep her temperature from rising. Her fever is raging at the moment."

A shiver rolled through Jane's body, and her brow furrowed once again. A quiet moan escaped her lips. Philip wished he could comfort her somehow, but he felt entirely helpless. He ran his hand through his hair, pacing in a circle before turning to Dr. Fernside. "Is that all?"

"She will likely awaken soon. Her body is fighting the illness with great resilience, I can see. She is quite exhausted. With plenty of water and rest she should recover, but it will take time."

Philip had never been more relieved. Emotion choked him, and he nearly embraced the physician with gratitude. Dr. Fernside stayed for a few minutes longer, instructing Jane's maid, Sarah, in how to properly care for her. Philip listened, memorizing each step, recording them in his mind for future use. He would not leave Jane's side until she was well and smiling again.

The physician took his leave, and Philip returned to kneel at Jane's bed. She had begun to stir, shifting restlessly on top of the mattress. She still shivered, and it took all of Philip's resolve not to cover her with blankets again. Her temperature needed to fall, but he hated to see her suffer.

When Sarah left the room, silence thrummed in the air. All Philip could hear was Jane's shallow breathing and his own racing heart. Worry still choked him, but he tried to dwell instead on the physician's optimism.

Miss St. Clair arrived to teach Jane, and Philip told her to return the following week instead. He gripped the hope in his heart that Jane would be well enough to undertake her lesson then.

Philip spent the morning hours beside Jane, where she remained in a deep sleep. In their solitude, and her lack of consciousness, he took the opportunity to speak the things he wished he could say to her. He confessed the extent of his feelings for her. He confessed that he loved her. Philip loved Jane, and he could not deny it. He declared his hope that she would one day care for him, his hope to build a marriage like the one his parents had shared—one of joy and deep, affectionate love, showing their children what it meant to love someone through deed and service, not just meaningless words.

If only he knew whether or not his words would be

well received by Jane. But her expressionless face, beautiful even amid her illness, showed no sign of comprehension.

By twelve o'clock, she still slept. The worry in Philip's heart grew with each passing moment. Sarah returned to the room, lines of concern marking her brow. "Shall we wake her? Dr. Fernside instructed that she drink plenty of water."

Philip stood from where he knelt on the ground, rubbing his sore knees. "I think we must try."

Sarah stepped forward. "Go on." She nodded at Jane, gesturing for Philip to make the first effort to wake her. His heart hammered with fear. What if she didn't wake? His mother's illness had progressed more quickly than his father's, and she had been larger than Jane, taller and not so petite. Philip recalled a day near the end of his mother's life, when she slept at all hours of the day, too tired and weak to open her eyes. He pushed the memory from his mind, refusing to imagine the same thing happening to Jane.

But terror still gnawed at his stomach as he leaned over her. His eyes stung. He had grown so accustomed to her smile and her laugh, he had never paused to wonder what he would do if he could never experience them again. His heart broke at the thought and he pushed it away, taking a deep breath.

"I'm sorry, Jane," he whispered as he slid his hands behind her.

Chapter 19

Sounds drifted to and from Jane's ears, like waves surging with the wind. She felt a touch, gentle like a flake of snow. Warm, much like the heat that burned throughout her entire body, interrupted by splashes of cold. Slowly the discomfort intensified, breaking through her consciousness like a sheet of ice.

The sounds began to come together, growing louder and clearer. Jane felt as though she were swimming up to the surface of the ocean, too tired to gasp for air. She felt herself rising, a persistent sound cutting through the rest.

Jane.

The voice, familiar and safe, was somehow connected to the touch at the back of her neck, the hand that gently shook her arm.

"Jane, do you hear me?"

Philip.

Her eyes opened, and everything came into clear focus. The sharp pain in her head, the burning heat of her body, the gnawing ache in her stomach, and the heaviness of her lungs. The warm, strong hand behind her head, and the other that cupped her cheek. She blinked, her half-lidded eyes surveying the face above her. She didn't like the grief and worry in Philip's brown eyes, but the moment she met them, they flooded with relief.

"Philip," she rasped. Her throat ached and scratched. "I do not feel well."

His eyes filled with tears and he smiled, giving an astonished laugh before burying a kiss in her hair. He drew back, gripping her hand. The room still spun, and she closed her eyes against the dizziness that swayed in her head. She could not be certain, but she thought she felt Philip's hand shaking as it held hers.

A glass touched her lips before liquid flowed into her mouth. She swallowed, the effort tearing at her sore throat.

Her breathing steadied, and the weight of her eyelids became too much to bear. Philip's hand was her only anchor to consciousness. When she felt it slipping away, she knew it was only in her mind. Philip would not abandon her.

The next time she opened her eyes, she found darkness. Her head pounded, and her heart raced. She tried to move but found the effort exhausting. Her entire body ached, each inhale taxing and every exhale forced. She lay on her back, unable to see anything but the crescent moon shining through her window. Her throat and lips felt as dry as parchment, and her clothes stuck to her skin with persistent sweat. She felt her blankets with her feet, hanging off the side of her bed. Chills erupted over her skin and she quaked with a rolling shiver. Exuding all her strength, she reached for the blankets. Her head pulsed with intense pain and her muscles refused to move. She had never felt more weak.

Frustration boiled inside her, coupled with her other magnified emotions. Tears leaked from her eyes as she tried to steady her breathing. She was completely alone, cold, and helpless.

Adjusting to the darkness, her eyes found the door between her chamber and Philip's. She couldn't walk to the door and she doubted her weak voice would reach him.

She sniffed, pinching her eyes shut against her tears. She felt like such a child, impotent and crying over a silly thing in the middle of the night. She couldn't move but she needed Philip. She didn't know why she needed him. What could he do to heal her? Nothing. The pain that extended through her body intensified with her quiet sobs.

"Jane?"

Her eyes flew open in the dark and a rustling of blankets met her ears. The tentative voice and the dim silhouette that sat up from the ground belonged to Philip.

"Philip?" she choked. She hardly recognized her own voice. What was he doing on her floor? She squinted against the pain in her head. His dark curls and wide eyes began to take focus as he knelt beside her bed.

"I didn't mean to startle you," he said in a gentle voice. "I couldn't imagine leaving you to sleep in here alone."

Jane hoped the darkness of the room was enough to hide her tears. "Thank you," she whispered.

Philip pressed his hand to her forehead, smoothing back her hair. Her eyes fluttered closed, and the pain in her skull seemed to melt away with every touch, every reminder that he was beside her.

"You are going to recover and become the greatest violinist in all of England," Philip said, his voice shaking. "Promise that you will."

Jane nodded before opening her eyes. Even with the lack of light, she could see the terror in Philip's eyes, the dread that shone there. The crease in his forehead, deepened by the shadows of the moonlight, struck her with a question, one that slipped from her parched lips without permission.

"Do you miss your family?" Her voice was nothing but a whisper. Philip had spoken briefly of his parents, always following the conversation with a light-hearted comment or jest. She had never learned how they had passed away, and she had never known how deeply it had affected him.

Philip traced his finger over her cheek, his jaw tightening. Through the moonlight in the window, Jane saw the tears in his eyes. "I miss them more than I can explain." He was silent for a long moment, and when he spoke again, his voice cracked. "When I saw you today… I feared I would lose you like I lost them. I do not know how I could carry on without you, Jane." He drew a shaking breath.

Jane had considered herself to be very unfortunate all of her life. She had been the least favored daughter, the awkward and undesirable debutante, and finally the recipient of an unwanted marriage. She had spent so much time pitying herself that she had often failed to notice the distant sorrow in Philip's eyes when he spoke of his childhood, of the parents he had loved so dearly. And lost so suddenly.

She thought of the statement she had made on their

first ride together at Pengrave. *Misfortune favors the wicked.* Jane could no longer believe that. Philip Honeyfield had suffered more misfortune than anyone deserved, and he was the best person she knew. What had she done to deserve him? She had once counted her marriage to Philip among her worst misfortunes, but her views had undergone a significant change in the recent weeks. He had become her dearest friend. Philip's hand still touched her face, burning through her skin, his eyes staring into hers.

"I promise I will live to be the greatest violinist in all of England," she said, her voice slurred and frail.

Philip gave a soft smile. "Will you leave any time for your husband? The presence of the greatest violinist in England would be in high demand, you know."

"Only if he promised never to throw food at me again," Jane croaked.

Philip's laugh, quiet and gentle, played against her heartstrings as her eyes drifted closed, a treasured lullaby to send her to sleep.

***

The days passed like weeks, and the weeks like months. Jane spent more time asleep than she did awake for the first week. Philip had brought an armchair into her room, where he spent his days reading aloud to her, telling her stories, and simply keeping her company. Through her window she could see the whiteness of the property, draped in endless snow.

By the end of the first week, she had recovered enough to venture to other areas of the house. She was not allowed by the physician (or Philip) to set foot outside, though she craved fresh, crisp air. She had developed a persistent cough, and in the nights that she was awakened by her cough, Philip immediately came through the door of his chamber, waiting at her bedside until she fell asleep once again. He often stayed beside her all night, sleeping on her bed beside her or on the nearby ground.

Her violin lessons were cancelled for three weeks while she recovered. One particularly snowy morning, she awoke alone. She rolled to her side but found her bed empty. The ground showed no sign of Philip either. With her regained strength, she climbed out of bed, reaching for the bell pull. Sarah arrived within minutes, offering her a warm cup of chocolate.

"How are you feeling this morning, my lady?"

Jane examined her reflection in the mirror behind Sarah. Her skin had developed a pink tone once again, her lips and cheeks rosy. Her cough had subsided over the last several days, and her temperature had steadied. "I am feeling much better."

Sarah smiled. "Oh, Master Philip will be quite pleased to hear that."

"Do you know where he is?" Jane asked.

"Yes! He is awaiting you in the library. He determined you would be well enough today to finish the story you have been reading together. I suspect he is planning a surprise for you as well."

Jane's eyes widened as she sipped from her cup, the hot, sweet liquid warming her from the inside. What could Philip be planning?

She had not had her hair arranged for weeks, and had taken to wearing her most simple, comfortable brown dress almost every day. Now that she was well again, she wanted to look as beautiful as she could. Philip had grown accustomed to her with matted curls and drab dresses, and she wanted to impress him. She smiled as Sarah began combing her hair.

When she finished, Jane studied the arrangement before thanking Sarah. They chose a pale blue gown to match her eyes. She drew a breath deep into her lungs, relieved to find them clear, the urge to cough finally gone.

Sarah stepped back, covering her mouth in awe. "You look lovely."

Jane thanked her, spinning in front of the mirror before exiting the room. Energy pounded through her with each step down the staircase. As she rounded the banister to the hall, she found Philip standing in the doorway of the library, a bright smile on his face as his eyes swept over her. He wore a deep burgundy waistcoat and a formal jacket, his crisp white cravat tied to perfection. It seemed his valet had made a vain attempt at arranging his hair, but the dark curls still fell endearingly over his forehead.

For a moment he just stood in silence, staring at her with enough admiration in his gaze to bring a blush to her cheeks. "How are you feeling this morning?"

"Quite well," she said, out of breath from her race down the stairs. She would need to ease herself slowly back into physical exertion after three weeks of rest. She eyed his clothing with confusion. He looked as if he were dressed for a ball. "You look... very elegant."

He threw his head back in laughter before straightening his collar. "Do you object to my elegance?"

She snorted back a laugh. "No... but I find it very uncharacteristic of you."

"I only had to ensure I could compare with your beauty this morning. I'm afraid I have still lost." His eyes shone with admiration as he smiled down at her. "I'm so glad you are well. I have never been more relieved. In celebration, it is my hope that you will agree to attend a Christmas ball this evening with me in Brighton. It will be hosted in the assembly rooms at eight o'clock, and the presence of the new Marchioness of Seaford has been heavily requested." He winked.

Jane's heart soared with excitement. She had nearly forgotten that the Christmastide was so near. She had always loved the season. Peace and joy and giving filled the hearts of so many, and celebrations abounded. Her birthday fell the week after Christmas, just before twelfth night. Amid the Christmas celebrations, her family had often treated her birthday as an unwelcome interruption, giving her a quick gift and promising to celebrate after the Christmastide. They rarely did.

"I would love to attend," Jane said.

Philip's face lit up before he cast her a look of concern. "Are you certain you're well enough? Do not feel like you are obligated to accompany me."

"I want to." She smiled to reassure him. "I haven't left Pengrave in weeks."

"The snow has been severe. We will need to leave plenty of time to reach the ball in safety, and we will need plenty of carriage blankets to wrap you in. I will not have you falling ill again."

She looked down at her feet, sudden emotion clutching her throat. "I wish to thank you, Philip. You did not need to look after me the way you did when I was ill. I don't know how I can ever repay you for your selfless service toward me."

He nudged her chin with his hand, raising her gaze to his. "It was not entirely selfless. I looked after you because I could not bear a life without you, Jane. I need you."

His quiet confession tore at her heart, breaking down

every defense she had built against him. His straightforward words and the sincerity in his eyes filled her with a warmth that spread through her bones. She needed him too, whether she had the courage to admit it or not. Her heart hummed with a secret, one that she had been avoiding. Her illness had stolen all clarity from her mind, leaving only her heart to be heard.

She loved him.

She loved the ungainly, ridiculous, and utterly adorable Marquess of Seaford. She loved his nearly constant smile, and his boisterous laugh, and his clear brown eyes. She loved his heart—the goodness within it. That it had been kind enough to choose her, even with all her imperfections.

Her weakened pulse gained strength as the realization poured over her.

Sparing her from a difficult reply, Philip stepped away from the door, ushering her inside. "Come now. I have refrained from reading the next page of our book for too long."

Jane shared a smile with him as she passed, her heart squeezing with an array of emotions. She could not continue hiding them for long. Each moment she spent with Philip threatened to overflow her hidden feelings. But why did she hide them? Why did she not confess that she too could not bear a life without him?

They spent much of the day in the library, and when the sun began to set, Jane excused herself to her bedchamber where Sarah awaited her to help her prepare for the ball. She found a new gown resting on her bed, the long skirts draping over the edge like a waterfall.

Sarah stood to the side, her lips pinched in a grin. Jane gasped as she stepped closer, in awe of the beautiful gown. She smoothed her hand over the emerald green fabric of the skirt, the silk cool and smooth under her fingers. Touching the beaded embroidery at the waist and neckline, she became certain she had never seen such a lovely dress. And she had certainly never worn one.

A set of matching slippers rested beside it, with a note pinned to them. Jane picked up the small slip of parchment, reading the words.

My dearest Jane,

A new gown for you is long overdue. Men do not usually think of these matters, and I see that I was very daft not to have a whole new wardrobe made for you when we first married. You might have reminded me, as it is your established responsibility to keep your husband from doing daft things. Don't you remember?

Jane grinned down at the note, signed in Philip's hand. She couldn't wait to wear the new gown, and she couldn't wait to see what Philip thought of it.

The pins in her hair needed only a slight adjustment, and Sarah chose an accessory to add to her head—a beaded comb to bury among her carrot curls. After dressing, Jane spun in front of the mirror, admiring the intricate detail of the deep green gown. It fit her figure perfectly, the color striking against her pale skin.

Jane breathed, willing herself to be confident. She had not yet ventured into public as a marchioness. She would prove herself to be a complete fool. Her heart thudded with nervousness. But Philip would be there, she reminded herself, beside her the entire night, and they could be fools together.

Jane grinned as Sarah placed the last pin in her hair.

Chapter 20

"Are you cold?" Philip asked Jane in the coach on the way to the ball. The sun had already fallen below the horizon, leaving just the light of dusk to guide them. Snow fell in gentle flurries from the sky, and the coachman drove slowly toward Brighton.

She sat across from him, bundled in at least three carriage blankets. Her face broke into a smile. "How could I possibly be cold with so many blankets?"

Her quiet laugh brought a grin to Philip's face. He shrugged in defense. "We must take the proper precautions."

"I am perfectly comfortable," she said, resting her head against the window. Her knees brushed against his as the coach rounded a curve in the road. Her lips pressed together in a smile.

Philip had thought he knew what it meant to be relieved. He had narrowly escaped many unfortunate situations in his past. But to see Jane well again had flooded him with peace and consolation like he had never felt before. He treasured her even more now. He hadn't thought it possible.

In the days that she had been ill, he had been given a great deal of time to think. If each hour, day, or week he had with Jane could be his last, what would he say? What would he do? He could not have her question his feelings with uncertainty, though he still questioned hers.

He would tell her how madly he loved her. He had decided the first week she had been ill, that he would finally confess his feelings to her candidly, in a manner that could not be confused for something less than the ardent love that he felt. But in the weeks that had passed since, he still hadn't said it. He did not want to scare her, or make her distance herself from him again. He treasured their time spent together, and he still could not decipher if she returned his feelings.

And he was afraid.

When they arrived at the assembly rooms, Philip helped Jane untangle herself from the blankets, laughing at the abundance of them. She took his arm as they approached the doors. Candlelight, ribbons, and greenery decorated the ballroom, the guests within the assembly dressed in their finest. Philip glanced down at Jane, noticing the unease that flickered in her gaze. "Why must they stare?" she whispered.

He covered her hand that held his elbow with his own, holding it tight against his arm. Her blue eyes jumped to his, and he offered a reassuring smile. "They are shocked that I managed to marry such a beautiful lady."

A shyness entered her expression as she smiled. Philip's heart crashed against his ribs.

"They are likely more shocked that you did not trip and fall on your way through the doors."

Philip gave a loud laugh, drawing even more gazes to their place near the deserted west wall. Jane covered her mouth with one gloved hand, hiding her giggle. A jaunty reel had begun in the center of the ballroom, and partners lined up in large quantities.

"We should make an attempt at sociality. Lord and Lady Seaford will be expected to be polite and grace the guests with their majesty." Jane grinned up at him.

He liked the way she spoke of Lord and Lady Seaford as if they were complete strangers. With her, he was simply Philip, and she was Jane. "You are right. But I confess I would rather spend the evening in solitude with you."

"The last ball we attended you promised me a dance," Jane said. "It never did happen."

"Because you led me away to find the music room." Philip raised one eyebrow with a smile.

Her cheeks darkened, the pink hue matching her lips as she moved her gaze to the floor. "Oh, yes. The mistake was my own, then."

He tilted his head down closer to her face. "Was it a mistake?"

She glanced up at him. His heart pounded in his ears, and he counted five seconds before she looked down again, unwilling to answer.

"I still do not fully understand why you led me there," Philip said.

Her posture tightened.

"You behaved as if you wished to be near me, as if you fancied me, even, yet you were so disappointed when your mother asked that I marry you." He could hear the hurt in his own voice, cutting through the softness of his words. He had been holding these questions in reserve for so long, afraid to receive the answers. He took a deep breath. "Were you only pretending?"

The dancers let out a cheer, calling Jane's eyes. When she looked up at him again, they were filled with guilt. She hesitated for a long moment, wringing her hands in front of her. "Yes," she said, her voice almost too quiet to hear. "I was deceitful and cruel. I was hoping to follow the Viscount of Barnet. I fancied him and hoped for a dance. I intended to utilize you to instill jealousy within him when he saw us together."

Philip felt as though he had been struck in the chest. He had suspected, but he had hoped he was wrong. He took a step back, the force of her words pushing him away without his permission.

She took a tentative step toward him, placing her hand on his arm. "Philip… that was before." Her voice shook. "Before I—"

Her eyes caught on something behind him, stopping her words. Philip turned, following her gaze. Her hand dropped from his arm.

"Lord Barnet," she said.

Philip's heart sank as the viscount stepped up beside Jane, his eyes narrowing down at her in warm greeting. Jane's eyes flicked to Philip before she gave Lord Barnet a bow, offering a smile. Inferiority twisted in Philip's chest, his heart pounding painfully around it.

"I trust you have been well these weeks?" Lord Barnet said to her, eyeing Philip.

"Indeed, very well."

"How is your family?"

"I imagine they are well," she said. "We have exchanged very few letters since they departed from Brighton."

Philip mumbled his excuses, walking away from their place at the wall. Every breath was painful as he crossed the ballroom. He didn't know where he was going, only that he could not stand to witness Jane speaking with Lord Barnet for another moment. She had appeared flustered beside the man. Did she still care for him? Her words to her mother in the music room pounded in Philip's ears, mingled with the vision of the tears that had rolled down her cheeks as she stared at Philip. *I don't wish to marry* him.

She had practically begged her mother to speak to Lord Barnet instead, to spare her the dreaded fate of a marriage with Philip. His doubt and uncertainty had faded over the past weeks, when Jane had laughed with him and talked with him willingly, and when she had admitted that she did not regret marrying him.

But she had pretended once before.

Had he been wrong to place his trust in the Claridges' advice? Would it have been wiser to keep his distance from her as he had the first part of their marriage? His heart had been fond of her then, but in the time he had spent with her since, she had claimed it as her own.

He stopped at the opposite wall, his jaw clenched against the emotion that hovered in his throat as he watched Jane and Lord Barnet across the room. She would have been happier with Lord Barnet. How could she not still resent Philip for taking away her choice? He had been foolish to assume that she would ever love him.

Hidden behind a crowd, Philip listened as the lively music ended.

Chapter 21

Jane had never known Lord Barnet to be so loquacious. Jane's reply to every question he asked was blunt, intended to end the conversation. She swept her gaze over the room for Philip but could not see him. Where had he gone? He had mumbled something about a drink but had been absent for several minutes.

"It is your birthday soon?" Lord Barnet asked, his voice low and, of course, brooding.

Jane nodded.

"How do you plan to celebrate?"

"My husband and I plan to make a trip to London for the theater." Philip had announced such a diversion as a potential celebration. But it would never happen if she didn't find out where he had gone. She craned her neck over the crowd.

"London is very crowded during the season," he said. "I would think your husband to be wiser than to choose such a crowded place. That is why I chose Brighton."

Jane scowled. "Brighton seems to be quite crowded as well."

"Yes."

Lord Barnet's disposition disturbed Jane. Harry's imitation of it flashed in her mind, and she found it to be shockingly accurate. Why had she been so drawn to Lord Barnet before? Her fascination with him felt like a distant memory now, faded so much that she wondered if it had existed at all. There was no question that he was handsome, but Philip was handsome in a much different way. Philip's expression was not mysterious, but bright and open. His eyes were brown, not ocean-green, but what they lacked in vibrant color they made up for in wit, joy, and expression. She could spend days in Philip's company and never grow tired of him, yet she was already painfully bored after minutes with Lord Barnet. When she examined her heart, she felt nothing for the man in front of her.

Nothing but annoyance.

"Please excuse me, Lord Barnet. I must find my husband."

He gave a nod as she turned away. She scanned the ballroom. Philip was taller than most, so it should not have been difficult to locate him. His head of dark curls came into view near the opposite wall, and she set off in his direction. He met her eyes as she approached, but his mouth did not smile.

"I have never really enjoyed assemblies," he said. "Especially not since becoming a marquess. Could I convince you to return to Pengrave early?" His voice came out cold.

Jane frowned, unsettled by the pain that hovered in his gaze. "Very well... is something the matter?"

He shook his head, offering a small smile that never reached his eyes. "Nothing. I simply despise large crowds."

"As do I, and as does Lord Barnet."

Philip's shoulders tensed, and he extended his arm for her to take. "Is that why he left the ballroom at Clemsworth?" A muscle jumped in his tensed jaw.

"I suppose so."

"But that was not why you left the ballroom at Clemsworth." He avoided her gaze as they walked, his voice quiet and full of hurt.

"Yes, but, I..."

"... do not need to explain." Philip looked down at her, moving a curl from her forehead, just as he always did. His touch burned as his fingers brushed her cheek. "I understand."

Jane suspected that he did not understand. She no longer cared for Lord Barnet at all. There was a time when she had been blind and foolish, but now her heart pounded with clarity. What she had felt for Lord Barnet had been a childish and outward infatuation, not love.

The ride back to Pengrave passed in silence, the space between them fraught with misunderstanding. Each time Jane opened her mouth to speak, she closed it again, fear stopping the words she wanted to say.

I honestly do not believe any man could fall in love with you, her mother's words struck her mind from a distant place, brought to life through the darkness of the carriage. Had her mother been right all along? Nothing could hurt more than speaking aloud her feelings for Philip and realizing that he, like her mother had believed, could never want her. He had given her countless reasons to believe otherwise, but her doubt was not easily dispelled. She had been trained her entire life to expect rejection.

When they walked through the doors of Pengrave, Philip bid her good night, carrying himself up the staircase to bed without waiting for her. Jane stood at the base of the stairs, tears stinging the back of her eyes.

As she prepared for bed, she stared at the door between her room and Philip's. He had slept in her room for the last three weeks as she had recovered. His wide armchair still sat against the wall beside her bed, his blankets folded neatly on the floor.

Crawling into bed, she pulled the covers to her chin. Sarah put out the last candle before exiting the room, leaving Jane to her thoughts. She rolled over, burying her face in her pillow. Tomorrow was a new day, a new opportunity to overcome her fear. She refused to let her days return to how they were before Philip befriended her. The early days of their marriage that had been filled with loneliness, misunderstanding, and hope for nothing but a bleak future. Tomorrow she would be brave, but tonight she needed to rest.

With firm resolve in her heart, Jane closed her eyes and tried to sleep.

White light seeped through her eyelids, and Jane had to blink twice to clear her vision. She glanced at her window, the red drapes contrasting with the thick white snow. Her heart leapt as she remembered her task for the day. She sat up, pushing her hair from her face. How would she say it? Would she simply blurt, *I love you*? No. She couldn't imagine being so outright.

She bit her lip, her gaze traveling to the door between their chambers once again. Could Philip still be asleep? She had risen early, so it was certainly possible. Tugging on the bell pull, Jane waited for Sarah to arrive. She had a brilliant idea.

A short minute passed before Sarah entered her room, a warm smile on her cheeks. "Good morning, my lady."

"Good morning, Sarah," Jane said. "I wondered if you might help me with something."

Her eyes widened. "Certainly, anything you wish."

"Will you request that Cook prepare an assortment of her scones? I wish to surprise Philip."

Sarah fiddled with the tie of her apron, her eyes focusing on everything but Jane. "Surprise Master Philip?"

"Yes."

"I'm afraid that will be quite difficult." Sarah's eyes shone with a secret.

"Why? I was certain that Cook would be happy to prepare Philip's favorite scones."

Sarah nodded fast. "Oh, she would, to be sure, but… Master Philip is not here."

"Not here?"

"I'm afraid not." Sarah chewed her lip.

Jane's scowl deepened. "Where is he?" She slid off her bed, wrapping her arms around herself to keep warm. Sarah noticed, hurrying to rekindle the fire in the hearth, avoiding Jane's gaze.

"I have specific instructions to not reveal his whereabouts." Sarah stuck the poker into the fire, turning a log. Bright orange sparks erupted from the dying flames.

"Who gave you these instructions?" Jane asked.

"Mr. Ambrose Curtis, and he received instruction directly from your husband."

The butler? Why had Philip confided his location in the butler and instructed him to keep it a secret from her? Had he run away? Returned to live with his grandmother in Brighton, leaving Jane to run the household alone? No, it couldn't be. "Has he gone to town?"

"I cannot say." Sarah kept her features free of expression.

"Please!" Jane begged. "At least tell me if I guess the correct answer."

"I cannot."

Jane collapsed on her bed, staring out the window. The snowfall had intensified, mingled with gusts of wind. "He should not be traveling in such severe weather."

Sarah's brow contracted in worry as she watched the snow. "Ambrose advised him against it but he insisted."

"Why must you keep it a secret from me?" Jane whined, clasping her hands together in a begging motion.

Sarah smiled. "If I told you it would ruin the surprise."

Jane sighed. Under any other circumstance she would have been excited. But the night before Philip had not been behaving in his normally jovial way. She had hurt him with her confession about Lord Barnet, and he had seemed aloof toward her. What if he had left only to escape her?

"When will he return?" Jane asked. "Will you at least tell me that?"

Sarah hesitated, replacing the poker by the fireplace. "Very well. I was told he would be absent for two days."

Jane jerked upright. "Two days?"

"Indeed."

She fell onto her back, fixing her gaze on the ceiling. At least she could spend the next two days planning the words she would say to Philip when he returned. It would drive her mad with curiosity if she was not informed of his location. How would she occupy her time without him? She glanced out the window again, worry settling over her, ominous and quiet. The snowy conditions were not safe to travel in. What could have compelled him to leave Pengrave in such weather?

She had been prepared to speak to him, to finally admit her feelings, but now she would have to wait. And Jane had never been patient.

Chapter 22

Arriving unannounced at the doorstep of Milton Manor had never been in Philip's plans. But here he was, shortly after nine in the evening, brushing snow off the rim of his hat as he struck his numb knuckles against the door. He stretched his legs and back as he waited for the butler to answer.

He had been traveling the entirety of the day to Ashford for one purpose: to retrieve Jane's horse.

The night before he had been restless, unable to sleep through the array of unsettling thoughts in his mind. He thought of paying the Claridges another visit for advice, but he decided he needed to find a solution on his own. If Jane did not love him after he brought her beloved horse back to Pengrave, he would accept that there was nothing more he could do. The moment the idea struck his mind, he had not been able to banish it. So he arose before the sun, informing Ambrose and Sarah of his surprise. Jane had described her home and its location in great detail one day, and Philip had taken note of the precise address. The weather had been potentially perilous, but he had determined the endeavor to be worth the risk. Her birthday and Christmas were approaching, and he needed to have the horse back to her as a gift.

The Milton's butler answered the door with a look of acute surprise, his heavily lidded eyes examining Philip. "Good evening."

"Good evening!" Philip said, hoping his cheerful voice and smile might serve to remedy his imposition. "May I request an audience with Mr. and Mrs. Milton? If they have not yet retired, of course. I am their son-in-law. Marquess of Seaford."

The butler's eyebrows rose as he ushered him inside and out of the cold. Philip waited in the entry hall for several minutes before a disgruntled Mr. Milton rounded the corner of the hall, followed by Mrs. Milton and a young boy.

"Lord Seaford!" Mrs. Milton exclaimed as she crossed the marble floor. Her eyes, wide with surprise, studied his face. "We did not expect your arrival. What has brought you here? Where is Jane?"

"She is at Pengrave."

Mrs. Milton shared a glance with her husband, a quiet chuckle escaping her. "She has already run him out of his estate." She returned her gaze to Philip. Her blue eyes sparked in the candlelight, her smile reminding him of a cat before a fresh dish of milk.

He pressed back his irritation, clearing his throat. "No. She doesn't know I have come. I mean to surprise her for her birthday by bringing her horse Locket back to her. It is my understanding that Locket was given to Jane as a gift. Would you allow me to bring him back to Pengrave? He is vital to her happiness there." He addressed Mr. Milton. "I offer one of my best horses in return. The black one on the right side."

"I see no reason why not," Mr. Milton said, glancing out the front window. "I will send a servant to trade the horses tonight and shelter them in our stables. May we offer you a room for the night, my lord?"

"I would be most grateful," Philip said.

Mrs. Milton pulled the young boy to her side. "Harry, meet the Marquess of Seaford."

The boy, likely no older than twelve, stared up at Philip with intense study, his freckled cheeks reminding Philip of Jane. It had only been one day and he already missed her. Harry, much like Jane, seemed shy upon first inspection, but Philip knew, due to Jane's stories of her brother, that he was not shy in the slightest. Philip smiled, bending closer to the boy's height. "It is a pleasure to meet you, Harry."

"Lord Seaford married Jane," Mrs. Milton said to her son. She gave another laugh. "I still cannot believe you agreed to marry her. No man has ever wanted her before. I have the utmost respect for you, Lord Seaford, and your choice to do the honorable thing by marrying our daughter."

Philip looked away from Harry, straightening to his full height. "The honor was all mine to marry your daughter, Mrs. Milton." He held her gaze, daring her to challenge his words.

He could imagine Jane roaming the halls of this home as a young child, her wide eyes sparking with freedom and joy. He imagined her smiles being swept away at the words of discouragement from her mother. Philip pressed down his anger.

Mrs. Milton cleared her throat, a high-pitched sound. "Yes, well, I am glad your feelings are as such. We will be happy to provide you with breakfast at ten o'clock before your departure in the morning. A guest chamber on the second floor should be prepared." She motioned for him to follow her to the nearby staircase.

He winked at Harry, throwing him a wide smile before following Mrs. Milton to the guest chamber. Shortly after he sat down on the bed, his small trunk was brought in. He fell back on the pillows, propping his hand behind his neck. What could Jane be thinking of his absence? The night before he had been awfully quiet toward her—the pain that throbbed inside him had been centered on her, and he hadn't trusted himself to speak. How could Jane ever want him when he had stolen her opportunity to marry a man like Lord Barnet? Philip had never felt more inferior to a man in appearance or grace. Philip wondered if Jane would even miss him, or care that he had left.

After another restless night, he arose and dressed early before glancing out the window of his room. Snow poured from the sky in large flakes, blowing at the house with vigor. Several inches of snow appeared to have fallen overnight. His hope fell. He had intended to travel back to Pengrave, but he had begun to question the wisdom of the idea.

He packed his trunk regardless, praying that the storm would cease.

When he met the Milton's in the dining room for breakfast, he sat across from Harry, adjacent to the boy's parents. Mr. Milton, uninterested in speaking with Philip, read from the *Times*, his spectacles balancing on the tip of his nose. A tray of eggs and ham was placed at the center of the table.

Philip met Harry's eyes as he reached for a slice of ham. Remembering Jane's warning, Philip prepared himself for the chance that Harry's ham might be thrown at his face.

"You cannot travel back to Pengrave in this dreadful weather, Lord Seaford," Mrs. Milton said, spreading jam on her bread. "Such an endeavor would likely render you injured or stranded in the snow."

"Ah, but the risk is well worth returning home this evening."

"Why are you so eager?"

"I miss Jane." Philip smiled, taking a sip from his glass.

Mr. Milton glanced up at him from behind his spectacles. "Do you now?"

"Indeed."

Raising both eyebrows, Mr. Milton exchanged a glance with his wife before returning his attention to the paper.

"I miss Jane too," Harry said around a mouthful of eggs. "I thought she was going to marry Lord Barnet and live here in Ashford."

Philip's stomach lurched at the mention of Lord Barnet. "I am sorry I took your sister from you." He gave Harry a look of sincere apology.

Harry shook his head hard. "I'm glad she married you instead. Lord Barnet is not nice and always looks like this." Furrowing his brow, he narrowed his eyes at Philip, his mouth a firm line. Philip laughed, deciding he liked Jane's brother immensely.

Mrs. Milton let out a long sigh. "I hope you are still able to live a joyful life, my lord, even with Jane always at your side. I understand she can be quite difficult to bear at times, and her constant prattle and singing can be irksome."

Philip dug his fork into his plate.

"I do apologize for her freckles. Despite my ardent effort to keep her out of the sunlight in her youth, she still developed an abundance. And her hair—"

"That will be quite enough."

Mrs. Milton's eyes flew open. "Pardon me?"

Philip's face burned under the heavy silence that had settled over the room. "I would ask that you do not speak of her in that way."

She sputtered. "She is *my* daughter."

"She is my *wife*. And I love her."

Mrs. Milton pushed her curls back from her face, her false smile hardening. "You love her?"

Philip stood from his chair. "I love everything about her. But I do not love the fact that she cannot seem to love herself. I have nowhere else to place the blame than with you, Mrs. Milton, her mother, for not loving her as she deserves."

She scoffed. "I love all my children."

"If you truly love Jane, you would not have reminded her of her shortcomings. You would not have constantly made her question her worth. You would not have forced her to marry me when she did not desire to."

Mrs. Milton stood, rage burning in her blue eyes. "How dare you question my devotion to my own child? I shared my opinions of her faults simply to help her remedy them. No man would have ever wanted her if she did not."

Philip pressed his hands down on the table, leaning toward Jane's mother. "*I* wanted her, and I always shall. Perhaps you might first consider remedying your own faults before inflicting your advice on Jane."

Mrs. Milton gasped, turning toward her husband.

He said nothing, turning a page of the *Times* as his wife seethed.

Considering Mrs. Milton's hospitality long spent, Philip excused himself from the table before she could speak another word.

Despite the severe weather, he would undoubtedly be unwelcome at Milton Manor for another night. He would need to leave now. He eyed the storm from the window of his chamber, apprehension gathering in his chest like the snow that piled on the trees. Undertaking the journey in a storm would take twice as long to return to Pengrave in safety, perhaps more.

He could not delay. Whether Jane cared for his safe return or not, he needed to see her as soon as possible, to give her the horse she adored. Her happiness was his sole purpose, and he knew the horse could bring her joy, even if he couldn't.

Picking up his hat, he exited the room, determination masking his uncertainty as he set off for Pengrave.

Chapter 23

It had been four days since the Christmas ball. Four days since Philip had left Jane on a secret errand. And four days without sleep.

Jane had never been so worried in her entire life. When the second day had passed, and Philip had yet to return, she had positioned herself in an armchair in the drawing room, facing the front window. She had found that watching the heavy snowfall did little to calm her nerves, haunting her mind with the most dreaded scenarios. Ambrose and Sarah had been unwilling to reveal his location to her, but she had seen the unease in their own eyes as they watched the ever-present storm.

After another night in the armchair, she awoke, blinking back tears as she stared between the panes of the window, desperately hoping to see Philip there. She had tried to keep busy during the days, but she could not clear her mind of the fear that he had abandoned her, or that he had been hurt in a carriage accident. Why else would he be gone for so long?

Imagining a future without him weighed on her heart, sending tears streaming down her cheeks as she tried to calm her mind. Her thoughts raced. What if she never saw him again? What if she could never tell him how much he meant to her? A gust of wind shook the windows.

"My lady?" Sarah's voice came from the doorway.

Jane turned, wiping her cheeks.

"Oh, dear, do not fret. Master Philip shall return." Despite Sarah's effort to hide it, Jane still heard the worry in her tone. The maid's eyes focused out the window. "Carriage accidents are not often fatal, though my great aunt was not so fortunate. She chose to travel in a storm much like this one, and her coachman was not accustomed to such conditions. Rounding a corner too swiftly capsized the coach. Crushed and killed by it, she was."

Jane bit back a sob, hiding her face in her blanket.

"But Master Philip is tall and strong," Sarah said in a quick voice. "He will not be so easily crushed."

"Will you please tell me where he went?" Jane asked, her words muffled by the blanket. "Please. Why did he leave? Did he mean to desert me forever?"

"Oh, heavens, no! I daresay he cares for you a great deal too much to desert you forever."

"Then where is he?" Jane looked up from her blanket, begging Sarah with her eyes. If Philip did return, his excuse for leaving would have to be very convincing. He had put Jane through four days of torturous curiosity and fear.

Sarah sighed. "If he has not returned by noon today,

I will consult Mr. Curtis. Perhaps we will come to agreeance that our promise to your husband may be broken. But it truly is a lovely surprise. I should hate to ruin it."

Jane did not care about a surprise. She wanted Philip back safely. Sarah coaxed Jane out of her chair, guiding her to her room to get ready for the day. Unable to eat at breakfast, Jane returned to her place in the drawing room. She brought a piece of embroidery with her but could not focus on the stitches. When the clock struck twelve, she called for Sarah and Ambrose.

"Where did Philip say he was going?" Jane asked again. The snow had begun to lighten, still falling, but with a new calmness.

The butler's thick brows furrowed as he exchanged a look with Sarah. After a long moment of silence, he turned his gaze to Jane. "Ashford," he said.

"Ashford?" What could have compelled Philip to travel to Ashford? Jane's mind raced, but she could think of no reason for him to go. "Do you know what has delayed him?" she asked.

Ambrose swallowed, his eyes dropping to the ground. "I'm afraid not."

Jane's stomach pooled with dread. The ride to Ashford only required a day, sometimes less. She lay her head on the back of the chair, fighting the emotion that squeezed in her throat. "Thank you for telling me."

Ambrose nodded. As he took a step away from Jane, his eyes widened, a smile creasing his face. "What fortuitous timing."

Jane followed his gaze to the window, her heart pounding. "What is it?"

He pointed to the drive, where a familiar carriage rolled over the snow. Jane jumped out of her chair, rushing to the window for a closer look. The moment the carriage door opened, a head of dark curls ducked out from inside, and Philip jumped down onto the snow. Tears sprung to Jane's eyes as relief flooded through her. The emotion lasted a short moment before anger clenched her fists. He was smiling—grinning unabashedly as he untethered the horses. Did he not realize how she had suffered in his absence?

Jane turned away from the window, marching out of the drawing room.

"My lady—" Sarah tried to follow, but Jane pulled open the front doors of the house before she could stop her. The cold bit through the long sleeves of her red morning dress, but the anger that pounded through her was enough to replace it. Trudging through the layers of snow, Jane pressed toward the drive where Philip stood beside the coach. He hadn't noticed her yet, intently focused on the horses.

"Philip Honeyfield!" She scooped up a handful of snow, throwing it at the back of his head.

He jumped, turning to her with wide eyes as the snow showered over his hair. The smile he wore had been wiped away, replaced with shock and confusion. "Jane, what are you—"

Another well aimed ball of snow struck him in the chest, and he turned away, laughing.

Jane's hands, numb and wet, fell to her sides. "It is not a laughing matter, Philip! How dare you leave me for days without explanation?" Her voice shook, quiet and weak as tears burned in her eyes. "I thought you had been crushed by your coach!"

He walked toward her, his boots leaving large prints in the snow. She sniffed, glaring at him through her tears as he drew closer. He shook his head, his brow furrowed. "I didn't think you would care."

"I was so very worried, Philip!" She blinked, clearing her vision enough to see his eyes, clear and open, the deep brown filled with astonishment and concern at once.

"You were worried about me?" he asked.

"Yes!"

"Are you certain?" He tipped his head down. His mouth still frowned in doubt, and his apparent confusion was too vexing to bear.

With one motion, Jane seized his face between her hands, pressing her lips firmly against his. He didn't move, apparently as shocked as she was by her own actions. Jane released him, her eyes rounding. Her cheeks burned as Philip stared down at her, his own eyes wide.

A beat of silence fell between them before he gripped her upper arms, tugging her to him. Before Jane could stammer an apology or explanation, he captured her lips with his, stealing the words from her mouth and her mind.

His lips, deliberate and urgent, moved over hers, his kiss deepening as he cradled her head in his hands. Jane held his jacket, the fabric bunching in her fists. Her tears fell, landing on Philip's cheeks and her own, the salt mingling with the taste of his lips. Her heart soared with belonging, warmth rising within her as Philip kissed her. She held onto him, afraid her legs had long lost their strength to stand.

His hand slid to the back of her neck, his touch burning through her skin, etching promises on her heart. Sliding her fingers into his hair, she returned his kiss with all the energy she possessed, with all the adoration she had been hiding. The moment she realized her breath was spent, she remembered she needed to tell him something.

"Philip," she gasped, only to have her breath stolen by another kiss, and another.

Her words could wait a moment longer.

At last Philip pulled away, lowering her heels to the snow. His eyes shone with awe, his quick breath visible in the cold air as he wiped the remaining tears from her cheeks. "Jane," he whispered.

"I must tell you something," she breathed, holding him at a distance so he could see her eyes. She could leave no chance for misunderstanding. Never again. "I didn't love Lord Barnet. Never. I did not know what it meant to love, or to be loved." Her voice cracked. "I love you, Philip. I love you more than anything."

His face tightened with emotion. He laughed into her hair, wrapping her up in his arms, holding her head to his chest. "I never thought I would hear those words."

She felt each steady and quickened beat of his heart against her cheek and closed her eyes. She had always considered herself to be short on fortune. But to know that Philip's heart belonged to her was enough to banish every misfortune she had ever faced. "I never thought I would speak them. I was too afraid to tell you I loved you. I have been the greatest fool in all of England for leading you to believe otherwise." She tipped her face up to his. "My mother favored you, and it created a prejudice in my heart. I was so very blind."

"I highly doubt your mother favors me now." Philip pressed his lips together, amusement shining in his gaze.

Jane narrowed her eyes, laughing. "What did you do?" She removed herself from his arms, remembering the anger that had brought her outside. "And why, pray tell, did you go to Ashford?"

He smiled without reservation, motioning to the horses at his right. Jane frowned, not catching his meaning. "What…?" her eyes caught on a black horse, its coat and face oddly familiar. She gasped. It couldn't be true. "Locket?"

"I hoped to surprise you for your birthday. But you caught me before I could hide him in the stables."

Jane covered her mouth, tripping through the snow as she approached her horse. She stroked his nose, bringing her hand to his muzzle where his whiskers tickled her hand. She sighed, running her hand between Locket's ears. Her heart surged with gratitude as she turned to Philip.

"You traveled all the way to Ashford to bring me my horse?" her voice was tight with the threat of tears. Raw joy enveloped her as Philip gave her a shy smile.

"It was nothing. Aside from the inn I was stranded at for two nights, the trip passed with ease."

She gave a hard laugh of disbelief, her heart threatening to burst with the love she felt for the man in front of her, for his goodness and kindness and countless other wonderful things. She had her entire life to spend finding even more things about him to love. He joined her beside Locket.

"Did my family receive you well?" she asked.

He rubbed the stubble on his jaw, his eyes igniting with a hint of mischief. "For a time."

"Philip!"

Laughing, he took her hands, warming them with his own. "Suffice it to say that my words to your mother were well executed and well deserved." His expression grew serious. "I want you to spend the rest of your life with the knowledge that you are loved, and treasured, and nothing short of beautiful." His eyes widened, as if he were just noticing the snow that fell all around them. "And I want you to remain in good health. It is far too cold out here."

His words nestled in her chest, finding a home in her heart where she would never forget them. She rose on her toes, wrapping her arms around his neck. Philip's arms moved to her waist, pressing her against him as he kissed her with renewed vigor. Before he pulled away, his mouth melted into a smile, and he whispered that he loved her against her cheek, trailing kisses along her jaw. Jane sighed, content to remain forever in his arms, even with the snow falling all around them.

She laughed as he bent over and scooped her legs off the ground, tucking one arm behind her knees and the other around her back. His laugh rumbled against her as she shrieked. She brushed the snow from his shoulders as he carried her toward the house, laughing at the hundreds of snowflakes that had gathered in his hair.

She glanced down at the ground, at the layers of snow and ice. "Please do not slip," she said, leaning her face into his neck. She closed her eyes, the image of Philip slipping on a patch of ice while carrying her all too realistic in her mind.

He gasped in mock offense. "The Marquess of Seaford is far too graceful to *slip*."

The moment the words passed his lips, he lost his footing. Jane cringed, clutching his shoulders as she squeezed her eyes shut. Philip gathered his balance, remaining upright. His laugh shook against her.

"My apologies."

"Philip!" Jane giggled until she couldn't breathe. Even in such clumsy arms, she had never felt safer and more loved.

Tipping her head back, she watched the snow above. It spiraled down from the sky like white petals upon them, a new and bright beginning. The snowflakes melted on her face. She listened to the peaceful crunching of Philip's feet in the snow and felt the gentle rise and fall of his chest as he breathed. The world was silent, serene, and beautiful.

Until Philip's feet flew out from under him, sending them both plummeting to the snow-covered ground.

Epilogue

There was nothing quite as charming to Philip as Brighton in the springtime, with the exception of his wife, of course.

He and Jane had been eagerly awaiting the day the snow would melt so they could ride to visit his grandmother and the Claridges. Like many things, Philip had learned, the change from winter to spring came gradually, one melted patch of snow, one blossom, one ray of warmth cutting through the dark clouds.

After mounting their horses, they set off for Brighton, in no hurry to reach their destination. Jane rode surprisingly slow, and Philip watched as she closed her eyes for a brief moment, letting the sunlight soak into her freckled cheeks. He smiled, catching her gaze as she opened her eyes.

"Is the spring in Ashford as lovely as this?" he asked.

Jane surveyed the surrounding ocean. A light breeze

rustled her hair, the sight still reminding him of autumn leaves. "Not quite so lovely, but charming in a different way."

"Do you miss it?"

Her gaze piqued. "Ashford?"

"And your family."

She lifted the reins as the path curved, silent for a long moment. "My home is here with you. But I do miss Caroline and little Harry. His mischief could rival even yours."

Philip chuckled. "When I met him he seemed perfectly well-behaved, and not at all inclined to throw ham at my face."

Jane's smile grew. "He is shy with meeting new people."

"Or you simply lied, and he is a perfectly dutiful child."

Jane's jaw fell in protest. "We established long ago that you were the liar." She waved one hand in the air dramatically, lowering her voice in a bad imitation. "'My horses understand the English language.'"

A laugh burst out of Philip and Jane snorted into laughter of her own.

Before their stop at his grandmother's home, they guided their horses to the Brighton coast, stopping off the edge of the beach near Clemsworth. Philip leapt down from his horse before helping Jane dismount. He let his fingers linger at her waist as he stared down at her. Framed by the ocean, her eyes gleamed bright blue as they smiled into his. Standing between Jane and the sun, he trapped her in his shadow.

"We could spend the day here instead," he offered.

Jane placed her palm against his cheek. "Your grandmother is expecting us. She would be quite worried if we didn't arrive as promised. I have experienced such feelings before." She raised one eyebrow at him.

He gave her a look of regret. "I am truly sorry for that."

She pressed her lips together, eyeing him with retained forgiveness, a glint in her eyes that led him to believe she was teasing. "You ought not to make your grandmother endure it."

"She will only miss us for a short time." Philip gazed down at her, a smile pulling on his lips. "I will blame the delay on you and your irresistible beauty."

She laughed as he clasped his hands together around her waist, inching her closer. He chuckled and lowered his lips to hers, a light touch at first, growing deeper as she welcomed his affection, pulling on the fobs of his waistcoat. His hands buried in her hair as he kissed her without reserve, undoing the pins that her maid had so carefully placed among her curls.

"I see you have wholeheartedly embraced my advice," a voice called from behind them.

Philip spun around, searching for the voice that could only belong to one man.

Lord Ramsbury sat on a nearby rock, tossing a handful of sand to the side with a wicked grin. When he had arrived, Philip couldn't say, but he seemed to have appeared out of nowhere.

Philip's face burned as he laughed. Pulling Jane to his side, he clasped her fingers between his. "Meet my wife, Lady Seaford."

"I had heard a rumor, but I couldn't believe it to be true." Lord Ramsbury stood, his balance less than stable as he sauntered toward them. Upon closer inspection, Philip saw the shadows under his blue eyes and the obvious neglect of a shave. His hair, dark blonde and normally well-groomed, fell messily over his forehead. "Philip Honeyfield, married to the woman he adores. If only we all could be so fortunate."

He flashed a smile at Jane before turning his lazy gaze to Philip once again. "I congratulate you, my friend. I am glad my advice served you well."

Philip could not believe the disarray of the man before him. Lord Ramsbury had never appeared so battered, the victim of a broken heart and an ongoing defeat.

"What advice?" Jane asked.

Lord Ramsbury opened his mouth to speak, but Philip stopped him.

"Nothing! Nothing at all." He threw Lord Ramsbury a warning with his eyes, to which he responded with a wink.

"I only ask that you place credit where it is due, Seaford. I am good for little of late." Lord Ramsbury rubbed his jaw, a flash of pain crossing his eyes, breaking through the devilish facade. With a bow, he turned away, leaving crooked steps in the sand.

"May I offer a piece of advice to you?" Philip called.

Lord Ramsbury cast him a glance over his shoulder.

"Do not throw your life to sea because you lost something you cared about. If I had chosen to do that, I would not be here today. I would not have found Jane."

Lord Ramsbury stared at him in silence for a long moment. As he looked away, he chuckled, running a hand through his hair. "As I said before, we cannot all be so fortunate." Raising a hand in farewell, he stumbled over the bank toward Clemsworth. Philip watched him, a weight settling over him as he witnessed the deterioration of his friend. He hoped Edward would one day find a love like he shared with Jane. It hurt Philip to see him so... uncollected and broken.

Jane squeezed Philip's hand, recalling his attention. "What was his advice?"

He gave her a wary glance, shaking his head with a smile. "I do not think it would be wise for me to tell you."

"Tell me!" she said, pulling on his sleeve. If he had learned anything about his wife, it was that she was unendingly curious.

He let out a long sigh. If he had been unsure of her devotion, he would have died with the secret. But he suspected Jane would laugh at the revelation now, attributing their kiss in the music room to the fateful event that had brought them together. He knew that deep inside, he was indeed grateful for Lord Ramsbury's advice, foolish as he had been to take it. He hoped the man would take his.

"If only to prove my honesty at last, I will tell you," Philip said, earning a smile from Jane. As he relayed the details, her eyes grew in size, until he suspected they might fall from her head.

When he finished, Jane shook her head in astonishment. "You followed advice from *him*? What could have possibly compelled you?"

That did seem to be the most common response. "It likely would have happened either way, the kiss. You were all too enchanting that night in the moonlight calling me 'vexing' repeatedly."

Jane threw her head back in laughter, a practice that she had developed from her time with Philip. "Well, it is true. You *are* incredibly vexing."

He chuckled, checking his surroundings for any watchful eyes before wrapping her up in his arms.

Find the complete series on Amazon

Brides of Brighton
A CONVENIENT ENGAGEMENT
MARRYING MISS MILTON
ROMANCING LORD RAMSBURY
MISS WESTON'S WAGER
AN UNEXPECTED BRIDE

About the Author

Ashtyn Newbold grew up with a love of stories. When she discovered chick flicks and Jane Austen books in high school, she learned she was a sucker for romantic ones. When not indulging in sweet romantic comedies and regency period novels (and cookies), she writes romantic stories of her own across several genres. Ashtyn also enjoys baking, singing, sewing, and anything that involves creativity and imagination.

www.ashtynnewbold.com

Printed in Great Britain
by Amazon